My Chocolate Year

A novel with
12 recipes

by Charlotte
Herman

illustrated by LeUyen Pham

Simon & Schuster Books for Young Readers

New York   London   Toronto   Sydney

SIMON & SCHUSTER BOOKS FOR YOUNG READERS

An imprint of Simon & Schuster Children's Publishing Division

1230 Avenue of the Americas, New York, New York 10020

SIMON & SCHUSTER BOOKS FOR YOUNG READERS is a trademark of Simon & Schuster, Inc.

Book design by Kristin Smith and Karen Hudson

The text for this book is set in ITC Cheltenham 11/17 pt.

The illustrations for this book are rendered in Japanese brush pen with digital shading.

Manufactured in the United States of America

2 4 6 8 10 9 7 5 3 1

Library of Congress Catalog-in-Publication Data

Herman, Charlotte.

My chocolate year / Charlotte Herman ; [illustrations by LeUyen Pham]. —1st ed.

p. cm.

Summary: In 1945 Chicago, as her Jewish family anxiously awaits news of relatives left behind in Europe, ten-year-old Dorrie learns new recipes in the hope of winning a baking competition at school. Includes recipes for various foods, from chocolate pudding to chocolate mandel bread.

ISBN-13: 978-1-4169-3341-0 (hardcover)

ISBN-10: 1-4169-3341-7 (hardcover)

[1. Baking—Fiction. 2. Contests—Fiction. 3. Schools—Fiction.

4. Jews—Fiction. 5. Family life—Illinois—Chicago—Fiction. 6. World War, 1939–1945—Fiction. 7. Chicago (Ill.)—History—20th century—Fiction.]

I. Pham, LeUyen, ill. II. Title.

PZ7.H4313Mxc 2008

[Fic]—dc22

2007037884

FIRST EDITION

In memory of my husband, Mel,
who introduced me to New York, chocolate egg creams,
and chocolate-covered Brazil nuts.

And for his namesake, Moshe Dov,
my new grandson.
I will introduce you to the same.

Acknowledgments

I want to thank Alyssa Eisner Henkin, my former editor, now agent, for her vision and amazing insights, and for helping me to make this book so much sweeter than just a story about chocolate.

And many thanks to my current editor, Alexandra Cooper, who so enthusiastically took over the reins and carried this book to completion.

To my recipe consultants, Janie Baskin, Marlene Brill, Sandy Goldstein, Charlene Regensberg, Lois Schnitzer, and my anonymous mystery baker, please come over and help me eat up all those brownies.

And finally, thanks to my son, Michael, and daughters, Sharon, Debbie, and Karen, always my enthusiastic readers and support team.

Safety Notice

Before making any of the recipes in this book, be sure to get an adult's permission. And always have adult supervision when using the oven or stove, and when using knives or other kitchen tools and appliances.

∾ Contents ∾

CHAPTER ONE

Sweet Semester, 1945

"Fifth grade with Miss Fitzgerald is going to be the best grade ever!" I said to my friend Sunny Shapiro as I tried balancing myself along the curb. "Imagine! Being in a real newspaper."

"And becoming famous!" said Sunny.

We were on our way home after our first day of school, still filled with the exciting news Miss Fitzgerald had given us just before dismissal.

"Class," she began, "even though it's only September, I want to tell you about a tradition that I follow every year at the end of the semester in January. Some of you might already know ..."

Before she even had a chance to finish the sentence, the kids shouted out, "Sweet Semester, Sweet Semester!"

Everyone in school knew about Miss Fitzgerald's popular event held each year.

"That's right, class. Sweet Semester. To celebrate the end of what I hope will be a sweet semester for all of us. And I'm telling you about it now so that you'll have plenty of time to prepare for it. Plenty of time to give it lots of thought."

She then went on to tell us what I already knew from my brother, Artie, who also had Miss Fitzgerald when he was in fifth grade three years ago.

Sweet Semester is a contest and here's how it works. We each bring in a dessert that we've made by ourselves, along with the recipe, and an essay about why we chose to make that particular dessert. Then everyone gets to taste each entry and vote on the winner. Miss Fitzgerald chooses the winning essay.

Just when I thought Miss Fitzgerald was finished telling us about Sweet Semester, she added something unexpected and wonderful.

"Class, this year, for the first time, I plan to invite a newspaper reporter and a photographer to come here and join us. And the winner—or winners—will have their pictures taken, and be written up in . . . the *Chicago Daily News*!"

The whole class went wild. We were yelling "Yippee!" and jumping in the aisles. And by the time the bell rang and we ran out of the building, Sunny and I could practically see our pictures right there in a major Chicago newspaper, shaking hands with Mayor Kelly.

"I just thought of something," I told Sunny as I hopped off the curb. "I can't cook and I can't bake."

"Come to think of it, I can't either," said Sunny.

"My cakes fall and my cookies look like pancakes."

"Same here, Dorrie. And don't forget. We have to write that essay."

"I'm not worried about writing the essay. I've got lots of erasers. But you can't erase a bad cake. I don't know what I'm going to do."

"Me neither," said Sunny, "but let's not worry yet. The end of January is a long way off. And in the meantime we can experiment."

"The one thing I know for sure is that I'll make something chocolate," I told her. "It definitely has to be chocolate."

"What did Artie make for Sweet Semester?"

"He piled three marshmallows on top of each other and called it a snowman."

"He made one snowman? How was that enough for the whole class?"

"It wasn't," I said. "And he didn't win either."

When I walked into the kitchen I found my mother pouring hot cocoa for Artie and me.

The cocoa was really good this time. Not like usual when she boils the milk so hot that skin forms on the top. There's nothing that makes me gag more than floating skin on top of milk.

"Miss Fitzgerald told us about Sweet Semester today," I said as I sipped the cocoa. "And guess what! This year the winners will get written up in the *Chicago Daily News*, with their pictures and everything."

"Ah, I can see it all now," said Artie, putting his cup down on the table and swiping the air in front of him in a grand motion. "Right on the front page . . . Dorrie Meyers wins Sweet Semester with pineapple upside-down cake!"

"I hate pineapple," I told him. "And I don't have to be on the front page. I'd be happy to see myself right in with the want ads. Or the crossword puzzle. I just want to make something wonderful. And original. Only I don't know what."

"I'm sure you'll think of something when the time comes," my mother said as she put on an apron.

"I can help you make a marshmallow snowman," said Artie.

"Great idea, Artie. But no thanks."

I brought my empty cup over to the sink and turned to Artie. "By the way, when you wrote your essay, what did you say about your reason for making a marshmallow snowman?"

"I wrote that marshmallows are fun to eat and almost everyone likes them and this was a unique way to make a snowman any time of the year and it wouldn't melt and you wouldn't even need any snow."

I shook my head and laughed. In a way, I wished I could be more like Artie. Not worry so much. Just do any old thing without thinking about it or caring, and whatever happens, happens.

While I was washing out the cup, my mother was rummaging in the cupboards, pulling out her Mixmaster, mixing bowls, measuring cups, and all kinds of ingredients. I could see she was getting ready to do some serious baking.

My mother is a wonderful cook and baker. She is famous for her carrot cakes. But today when I saw her taking out the jar of honey, I knew what she was getting ready to bake. A honey cake for Rosh Hashanah—the

Jewish New Year. And this would be our first Rosh Hasha-nah since the war with Germany and Japan ended.

I love celebrating Rosh Hashanah, when relatives come over. We eat all kinds of sweet foods. Sweet kugels, sweet carrots, apples dipped in honey, and of course, my mother's honey cake. Sweet foods for a sweet year.

I think honey cake is okay for the adults. They seem to like it. But for me there is nothing like chocolate.

"Do you think you could bake a chocolate cake while you're at it?" I asked my mother.

"Another time," she said. "I'm so far behind. And there's so much I have to do yet."

So I just hung around and watched as her hands worked their magic: measuring, sifting, pouring. I thought maybe if I watched real hard every time she baked, really studied, I could learn something.

Maybe some of her magic would rub off on me.

CHAPTER TWO

Rosh Hashanah

Crash! Bang!

"No, no! Get away!" My mother was screaming from the kitchen.

At the sound of the crash Artie and I ran in from the dining room where we had been playing with my Uncle Jack's dog, Buddy. But Buddy got there first and in a flash he was attacking my mother's pot roast lying on the floor.

"No!" yelled Uncle Jack. "Drop it!" With one hand he grabbed Buddy's collar and tugged at him while my mother pulled the roast out of his mouth.

And as Buddy was lapping up the carrots and onions and gravy from the linoleum, my mother was drying her tears with her apron.

Artie and I cleaned up the floor with some wet rags, but there wasn't much to do because Buddy pretty much cleaned it up for us. He just stood there licking his mouth and wagging his tail like it was the best meal he ever had.

"You crafty canine," Uncle Jack said to Buddy. "Stop looking so smug."

Buddy is a black-and-white English springer spaniel with adorable floppy ears. Spaniels are good hunting dogs, so I guess that's why he was so quick to get at the pot roast.

"I don't know how it happened," my mother said. "The pan just slipped out of my hand." She sank into a chair.

"Don't worry," said Uncle Jack. "I can go out to the butcher shop and see if they have any more meat."

Even though the war was over, there was still a shortage of meat. And sometimes it was hard to get.

"No, don't bother," she said shaking her head. "There won't be anything left. And I have plenty of chicken." She let out a deep sigh. "I just don't know where my mind is lately. I can't concentrate on anything."

Uncle Jack sat down at the table next to her. He had stopped by earlier that Thursday saying he was in the neighborhood, walking Buddy. But I think he came over to sample some of my mother's cooking. He knew she was preparing for our big meal on Friday night. I guess he didn't count on Buddy doing the sampling too.

"I can't tell you how worried I am," my mother said as she sipped a cup of tea and wiped away some more tears. I didn't think the tears were just because of the roast.

They sat at the table, close together, talking softly. But I could still see and hear them from across the kitchen where I was gathering up the wet rags.

"I'm worried too," said Uncle Jack, digging into a piece of sweet noodle kugel. "The last letter I got from them was way back in 1941. I remember because it was the year I bought the Plymouth."

It's well known in our family that Uncle Jack, who is my mother's brother, measures time by his 1941 Plymouth. Everything that's ever happened in his life is either BP or AP. Before Plymouth or After Plymouth.

"That's when I last heard from them too," my mother said. "And ever since the war ended I've been sending letters to anyone I can think of, trying to find out what happened. Four months already and I haven't gotten any answers."

"What letters are you talking about?" I asked, recovering a stray carrot from under the table.

"Oh, we're just talking family talk," my mother said, which is what she always says when she thinks I'm not old enough to understand something.

"Well I'm family too, aren't I?" I took Buddy by the collar and led him back into the dining room. "Come on, Buddy. I guess we know when we're not wanted."

On Friday night the relatives came to celebrate the new year. Bubbie—my grandmother—came with Uncle Jack and Aunt Esther, who is my mother's sister, and a pot of stuffed cabbage. Uncle Louie and Aunt Goldie, who are on my father's side of the family, brought sweet and sour meatballs. Nobody brought anything chocolate.

When we sat down at the table, my father said the blessings over the wine and challah bread, and passed around slices of apples that we dipped into honey.

"*L'shanah tovah!* To a good year!" we wished one another. "May we hear good news from Europe."

My mother and Aunt Esther carried in the steaming bowls of chicken soup, and Artie and I helped bring in the roasted chicken, sweet carrots and kugels, the stuffed cabbage, meatballs, and salad. There was so

much food—even without the pot roast—that we had to take the vase of flowers off the table to make room.

Everything looked delicious. "I'm starving," I said to Artie as I started to fill my plate. I didn't think anyone else heard me. But Aunt Goldie did. She was sitting right next to me.

"Sweetheart, what do you know from starving?" she said. "The children in Europe . . . *they* are the ones who are starving."

She said that to me just as my fork was about to pierce a second meatball. I had counted on a third one, too. I love sweet and sour meatballs. And stuffed cabbage. But now, after Aunt Goldie said that, I lost my appetite. How could I fill up my plate with all kinds of wonderful food when children in Europe were starving? So I just took a small piece of chicken and a spoonful of carrots.

"That's all you're having?" Aunt Goldie said when she saw my plate. "Sweetheart, take something else. No wonder you're so skinny."

I can never understand why some of my relatives keep reminding me that I'm skinny. Like I don't already know.

"Maybe later," I told her.

While we ate, the subject of the letters came up again. The conversation started in English but quickly and quietly switched to Yiddish. As if Artie and I couldn't understand what they were talking about.

When we were small and my mother and father didn't want Artie and me to understand what they were saying, they'd speak to each other in Yiddish. And many of my relatives often speak Yiddish when they get together, especially when they get excited about something, like when they get into an argument. Didn't they realize that somewhere along the way we figured them out? That by now we could understand them?

I pretended to be studying the bubbles in my glass of ginger ale and Artie concentrated on the chandelier above the table.

I listened to them talking about the letters they had been waiting for but weren't receiving, and talking about Bubbie's sister, Sophie, from Lithuania. And then more names: Mina and Joseph and their son, Victor. I knew that Victor was a distant cousin of mine. A second cousin, I think.

Bubbie sat quietly, pushing the meat and rice around on her plate with her fork, listening to the conversation.

"We would have heard something by now. It can't be good."

"Europe is in so much chaos. It's too early to know anything about anybody. People are scattered all over."

What happened to Sophie? And Mina and Joseph and Victor? Hearing all this talk about them made me think of a newsreel I saw one time.

A few months ago I went to the Central Park Theater on Roosevelt Road with my mother and father to see a movie starring Esther Williams. She's a fantastic swimmer. But what I can't understand is how she can swim and do ballet underwater and still come up with dry hair. And how can she breathe and smile at the same time?

Anyway, what I remember more than the movie was the newsreel: "The Eyes and Ears of the World." It was all about Hitler, and Germany surrendering. And it showed American soldiers and German soldiers, and huge ovens and ashes all around them. And the people in the theater were crying. My mother and father, too.

Usually my father likes to go out to a restaurant after a movie. He loves restaurants. My mother doesn't. She always says she can make anything better and cheaper at home. But this time, even my father didn't want to go out to eat.

"What was that all about?" I asked when we left the theater. Nobody said anything. They just put their arms around me as we walked home together. But I didn't need to ask them. I knew what I saw. I saw ashes. The ashes of people who perished in the war.

CHAPTER THREE

My Mother's Bridge Club

The synagogue hummed with the Rosh Hashanah prayers on Saturday and Sunday. I sat up in the balcony with my mother and listened to the cantor chant the most beautiful melodies. And when the rabbi spoke of all the Jews who were killed in Europe, women cried into their handkerchiefs.

"And many of those who survived are broken in body and spirit," he said. "They have lost everything. Their homes and their families. They have nowhere to go."

When he spoke about all those people who didn't have families anymore, I leaned in closer to my mother and thought about how lucky I was to have her. My father and Artie, too. They were sitting downstairs with the men. I wondered if any of the men were crying.

On Sunday I heard the blowing of the shofar, the ram's horn, and goose bumps sprouted on my arms. I knew the sound was to make us think about the year gone by, and to look ahead to the new one.

At times I studied the ladies' hats. Large hats. Crazy hats. With flowers and feathers, or even fruit. And I knew that I would never wear hats like those when I grew up. Why would I ever want to walk around with fruit on my head?

It seemed that Rosh Hashanah put my mother in a quiet, thoughtful mood. So I was happy to see how she brightened up a few days later when she made her announcement.

"My club is coming over tonight. I need you to help me clean up."

"Club?" I asked. "Since when do you belong to a club?"

"My new bridge club. The girls and I have decided to get together once a week to play cards. I'm having the first meeting."

My mother set out little dishes filled with chocolate-covered candies of different shapes and sizes.

"Don't eat any of the bridge mix," she said. "I need to make sure there's enough for tonight."

"You mean they make candy especially for people who play bridge?" I asked. "Then why don't they make candy for people who play Monopoly and checkers?" I aimed my hand toward one of the dishes. "Can I have just one piece?"

"All right. Just one."

I picked out the biggest piece of candy I could find. It was round. I bit into it and discovered a chocolate-covered malted milk ball. It reminded me of the malteds I get at Ziffer's Drugstore. I wanted another one.

"Can I have just one more?" I asked.

"If there's any left after tonight you can have some tomorrow."

When the girls came over, Artie and I hid in the room we share. We could hear them through the walls. They were talking very loudly. They were laughing. They were cackling.

"Like witches," Artie said.

"Like chickens," I said.

My mother was cackling right along with them. I could tell she was having a good time.

As I listened to their voices something occurred to me. "You know, everyone except Ma has an accent—from Europe," I told Artie.

"Ma has one too," Artie said.

"No she doesn't."

"Sure she does. And so does Dad."

I listened really hard, but I still couldn't tell.

"I think you're imagining it," I told him, and I flopped down on my bed. "All I know is they'd better save us some of the chocolate-covered malted milk balls."

"And the chocolate-covered peanuts and raisins," said Artie.

We waited for them to go home. But they didn't. Their laughing and cackling filled the air as I drifted off to sleep, praying that they wouldn't eat up all the bridge mix.

There was plenty of bridge mix left in the morning. My mother said I could take some for recess. So I took the malted milk balls and Artie took the peanuts and raisins.

After school my mother let me help her cook the chocolate pudding that we were having for dessert at supper time.

I love chocolate pudding. It's so rich and smooth and chocolaty. And I love cooking it, too. I like the way it thickens and bubbles as it gets hotter and hotter.

"Ma," I said as I was stirring, "do you have an accent?"

She came over and set down the cups she'd brought me for the pudding. "I suppose I do. Why do you ask?"

"Well, last night Artie said you have one. And that Daddy has one too. But I never noticed."

I poured the pudding into the cups and my mother put them in the Frigidaire to cool. Then I sat down at the table with the pot to lick whatever was left of the pudding. First with a spoon, then with my finger. I wondered if chocolate pudding would be good to bring for Sweet Semester. Probably not, I thought. Too ordinary.

"I mean, you don't sound like the ladies—the girls— from last night," I continued. "Or the neighbors. And you sure don't sound like any of the aunts and uncles, like Aunt Goldie or Uncle Louie."

My mother sat down across from me. "That's because they were older than I was when they came from Europe to America. The older you are when you come to a new country, the harder it is to lose the accent."

My hands and face were messy from all that licking and scraping, and just as I was getting ready to clean up, Artie came home. When he saw me he laughed and called me a chocolate-covered Dorrie.

"Very funny," I said as he ran off. I went to the sink to wash up and said, "So, Ma, how old were you when you came here, anyway?"

"I was fourteen. The oldest of my brothers and sisters. And Uncle Jack was the youngest. He was just five. So that's why he doesn't have an accent."

That evening at supper, as I dug into the cold, thick chocolate pudding and slowly licked off each spoonful, I listened closely as my mother and father were talking. And I discovered something. They actually do have accents. Funny how I never noticed before.

How to Make
Chocolate Pudding

INGREDIENTS

1/2 cup sugar
3 tablespoons unsweetened
  cocoa
1/4 cup cornstarch

1/8 teaspoon salt
2 3/4 cups milk
2 tablespoons unsalted butter
1 teaspoon vanilla

WHAT TO DO

In a saucepan stir together sugar, cocoa, cornstarch, and salt. Place pan over medium heat and stir in milk. Bring to a boil. Cook, stirring constantly until mixture thickens. Remove from heat and stir in butter and vanilla. Pour into cups.

You can let it cool a little and eat it warm. Or put it in the refrigerator and eat it later. If all this seems like too much work, just buy the chocolate pudding that comes in a box. That tastes good too!

CHAPTER FOUR

Swell September

Usually after the first few days of school in September, school starts to get pretty boring. But fifth grade with Miss Fitzgerald was really swell. She made everything interesting. Every day she brought in newspapers and magazines so we could discuss what was happening around the world.

One day she brought in a photograph she cut out from a magazine and held it up in front of the class. It showed four small children in ripped and dirty clothes sitting in the ruins of a bombed-out building.

"Just look at these children," Miss Fitzgerald said. "They are just a few of the many children who are now homeless and hungry because of the war. Countless numbers of children were orphaned by the war, too. Maybe even these very boys and girls you're looking at now."

Our classroom, usually busy and buzzing with note-passing, whispers, and pencil-sharpening, was totally silent. Even the talkers, like Estelle Goodman and Freddie Bass, had nothing to say.

Miss Fitzgerald passed the photograph around so we could get a better look at it. Up close you could see the sadness in the children's eyes.

The photo reminded me of a movie I once saw called *Journey for Margaret*. It starred Margaret O'Brien, who is a very famous child actress. In the movie Margaret plays an orphan who lives in London during the war.

It's a movie I never forgot because it was so sad and I cried so hard. I even cried when Margaret finally got adopted by Robert Young and Laraine Day, who played her new and loving parents. And now here I was looking at pictures of kids who could have been real orphans.

"What do you think we might do to help these children?" Miss Fitzgerald asked. The room was buzzing again and the answers started coming.

"We can send food," said Rosalyn Russo.

"Food can spoil," said Freddie Bass. "We should send money."

"And how can we get the money?" Miss Fitzgerald asked.

Estelle Goodman said we should sell lemonade. But Melvin Freid said that people will only buy lemonade in the summer and we should have a bake sale instead.

"But we're already having Sweet Semester," I said. "We can't have a bake sale too."

"Maybe we can," said Miss Fitzgerald. "I've been doing some thinking. What if we make Sweet Semester really big this year? What if we were to invite parents and guests? And we were to ask everyone who comes to donate some money to a food fund that we set up? Then we can send the money we raise to a charity that helps hungry children overseas. This could be the most meaningful Sweet Semester of all time."

We were getting so excited about having the most meaningful Sweet Semester of all time that we started shouting, "Yeah, let's do it! Let's do it!" And I bet if our chairs weren't bolted to the floor we would've all tipped over and fallen out of them.

"I think it would be a good idea if each of us could also contribute to our food fund," said Miss Fitzgerald. "So start saving your pennies."

"Now," she said as she returned to her desk, "how many of you have already decided what you're going to make for Sweet Semester?"

I glanced around the room and saw that more than half the class had their hands raised. Sunny and I looked at each other and shrugged.

"That's wonderful, class. And I'm sure the rest of you will come up with something soon."

"Can parents help?" Estelle Goodman asked.

"They can help, but you have to be the one to actually prepare the dessert. And be sure to get permission to use the stove and other equipment. Remember, even though the war has ended, there's still sugar rationing, so ask your mothers before using it. You want to be careful not to waste any."

"Can two people go in on something together?" Freddie Bass asked.

"Only if it's something spectacular. And I want to know about it beforehand. Otherwise you are each to do your own."

The questions kept coming.

"What happens if there's a tie? Like two people win for the best recipe or the best essay? Or one person wins for both? Who gets to be in the *Chicago Daily News*?" Rosalyn Russo asked.

"Any and all winners will be in the paper."

I really wanted to get my picture in the paper. I could

imagine my mother showing it to the girls in her bridge club. And my father bringing it with him to work and showing it off. Everyone would try my winning recipe. Or read my winning essay.

I could even see myself writing for the newspaper someday. I could be a reporter and walk around with a little notebook and write about all the interesting people that I meet. I really wanted to win. And I wanted Sunny to win too.

"Wouldn't it be great if we could both win?" I said to Sunny on the way home. "If we tied for the best recipe? Or the best essay?"

"Or you could win for one and I could win for the other," she added. "Or we could go in on something together because it'll be spectacular?"

"Gosh," I said, "so many kids already know what they're making. Did you see how wildly Melvin Freid was waving his hand? I wonder what he's planning to make. It must be something special. He's such a great artist."

"But this contest isn't about art," Sunny said.

"But he decorates his own birthday cakes."

"But does he bake them too? That's the question."

When I got home I looked for an idea for Sweet Semester in a few of my mother's *Good Housekeeping* magazines, but I didn't see anything I liked. Then I checked my *Betsy Belle*. I love *Betsy Belle*. It comes out once a month and it only costs one dollar for a whole year.

My mother always tells me that I could be a model in that magazine if I wanted to. But I don't think I could. Even though most of the girls in there wear braids like I do, none of them have tree branches for arms and chicken legs. And I bet they don't have trouble keeping their blouses tucked into their skirts and slacks like I have. My mother says it's because I don't have a waist yet.

I looked through the magazines, in the part called "Betsy in the Kitchen," but there was nothing interesting there either. And then I saw Margaret O'Brien (who also wears braids), advertising the Margaret O'Brien Candy Kitchen. It's a kit where you can make your own lollipops. At first I thought maybe Sunny and I could get one, but decided it wouldn't be fair to use a kit. We were supposed to make something on our own.

And I wanted mine to be original and wonderful. I hoped I would come up with an idea soon.

CHAPTER FIVE

Chocolate Malteds

One of the best places to get a chocolate malted in all of Chicago is at Ziffer's Drugstore on Independence and Douglas boulevards. At least that's my opinion. The malteds are thick, you get a lot, and they only cost a quarter.

"After seeing that picture of those hungry kids yesterday I feel kind of guilty about spending my quarter on a malted," I told Sunny as we walked to Ziffer's after school. The day was warm with lots of sunshine and we didn't have too much homework. It was a perfect day for a malted.

"We won't be getting them much longer with winter coming before we know it," said Sunny. "We'll be able to save up plenty of quarters for the food fund."

My mind found its way back to *Journey for Margaret*.

"Sunny," I said as I walked along trying not to step on the cracks in the sidewalk, "do you remember when your mother took us to see that movie where Margaret O'Brien was an orphan during the war and was finally adopted by Robert Young and Laraine Day?"

"Gee, how could I forget? We ate Raisinettes and cried at the same time. I think I even got the raisins wet."

"I wonder how she was able to act so believable."

"Like she really *was* an orphan," Sunny added.

"And how did she make herself cry? You really have to be a good actress to cry on command."

"She's good all right," said Sunny. "That's why she won an Academy Award for *Meet Me in St. Louis.*" We grabbed hands and ran the rest of the way to Ziffer's, stopping just once when I spotted a shiny silver penny lying on the sidewalk.

"Here," I said handing the penny to Sunny. "For your silver penny collection." Silver pennies came out a couple of years ago when there was a shortage of copper. Artie said the coins aren't really silver. That they're just steel coated with zinc. But to me they look like silver. And they're beautiful. I have a batch of silver pennies in my dresser drawer, but Sunny has a whole jarful.

"This makes one hundred silver pennies exactly," said Sunny.

By the time we got to Ziffer's, my blouse had sneaked out of my skirt. So I tucked it back in before I plunked myself down on a stool next to Sunny at the soda fountain and slapped my quarter onto the marble counter.

"Two malteds, please," we called to Frank, the soda jerk who was wiping up the counter with a towel. I liked the way he looked in his white hat and long white apron.

Frank never asks us what flavor we want anymore. He knows us by now. He knows we just like chocolate.

Sunny and I watched as Frank took two tall metal containers from a shelf. Into each one he dropped three scoops of ice cream, added chocolate syrup, Horlick's malt, and milk. Then he attached the containers to the mixers and turned on the motor.

While the motor whirred, we twirled around on our stools. Whirring and twirling. And when the whirring stopped, so did the twirling. Frank poured the thick, creamy malteds into our glasses and topped each glass with whipped cream. There was plenty of malted left over in the containers for second helpings. He brought us each a packet of two vanilla wafers for eating, and two straws for sipping.

Sunny took a sip. "Mmmm, sweet."

"And chocolaty," I said. "Mmmm."

"You're so lucky," said Sunny in between sips. "You can drink all the malteds you want and never gain any weight. Every time I drink one, another button pops."

"Lucky? Did you ever take a good look at my tree branches and chicken legs?"

"Still, I'll trade with you anytime," she said.

So there we sat, sipping malteds together like we've done a hundred times before. Sunny is my very best friend. We do just about everything together. We walk to and from school together, we do homework together, and go to the movies together.

Almost every Saturday morning we're either at the Central Park or Lawndale theaters, stuffing ourselves with Goobers, Raisinettes, and Milk Duds, and laughing at Abbott and Costello or crying at the end of *The Fighting Sullivans* when all five Sullivan brothers get killed when their ship is sunk by the Japanese.

Sunny Shapiro is actually Sonja Shapiro. Sonja—like

the famous ice skater, Sonja Henie. But she doesn't like that name, so she calls herself Sunny. She even looks sunny, with her short blond hair and freckles sprinkled across her nose.

Sunny and I became friends one morning during my favorite part of first grade—milk and cookie time.

When the monitors came into the room with the giant brown box of cookies and the crate of small milk bottles, I got so excited—until I remembered that I had no money. No money for a bottle of milk that I could drink with a straw. No money for a chocolate-covered marshmallow cookie with a pecan on top.

I watched as the other kids walked up to the front of the room with their milk money. Watched as they took one of the small bottles of milk and watched as they took one or even two chocolate-covered marsh-mallow cookies with the pecan on top.

I couldn't bear to watch them eating and drinking, so I covered my face with my Dick and Jane book, *We Look and See*—the red one with the soft cover. That's when I heard a voice.

"What's wrong?"

I looked up and saw Sunny. She was standing in front of me holding a bottle of milk and a cookie.

"Nothing," I said.

"Then why are you holding your book upside down?"

I shrugged and put the book away. "I forgot my milk money," I finally told her.

Sunny put her bottle of milk on my desk, broke her cookie in half, and the nut too, and gave me half of each. Then she went to get an extra straw and we took turns sipping.

After school I told my mother what Sunny had done for me. "That shows fine character," she said. She took some change out of her coin purse and gave it to me for the next day so I could treat my new best friend to milk and cookies.

Now we were enjoying the last few drops of our malteds, making loud slurping noises through our straws and laughing ourselves silly.

"Maybe I can bring chocolate malts for Sweet Semester," I said.

"Not original," said Sunny. "Anyone can make a malted."

"It's not as easy as you might think," I told her.

How to Make a Chocolate Malted

If I don't have a quarter to buy a malted, I make one myself.

Like Sunny, you might think it's easy to make a malted. Just mix ice cream, milk, chocolate syrup, and malt all together, and that's that. But there's more to it.

If you like your malteds thick, like I do, you have to use a LOT of ice cream and very little milk. But if you like them thin, you should use less ice cream and more milk.

Here's how to make a thick chocolaty chocolate malted. So thick that the straw stands up in the glass!

In a blender, combine:

INGREDIENTS

3 large scoops chocolate ice cream
3/4 cup milk

1/2 cup malt powder
2 tablespoons chocolate syrup

WHAT TO DO

Blend it all together until it's thick and foamy. Pour it into a tall glass, put in a straw, and sip away! This will be enough for you and a friend, or you can have seconds. (And don't forget to put the top on the blender!)

CHAPTER SIX

A Weekend with Bubbie

Sometimes on a Saturday, my mother goes downtown. She hardly ever goes during the week. She's too busy cooking, cleaning, washing and ironing, and shopping at the butcher, the fish store, and the A&P.

But on Saturdays she doesn't do any of those things. She puts on a nice dress and relaxes. And sometimes she'll go downtown to Marshall Field's or Carson's or the Boston Store.

When that happens, I spend the day with Bubbie. And sometimes I stay overnight.

Bubbie is my mother's mother. She doesn't have an accent. You might ask, how can that be? If my mother has an accent, and she's younger than Bubbie, how come Bubbie doesn't have one? Here's the answer. Bubbie doesn't speak English. She can understand it but she can't speak it. She speaks Yiddish.

I, on the other hand, can't speak Yiddish. But I can understand it. And that works out just fine. I speak to her in English, and she speaks to me in Yiddish. I love it when she gets all excited about something and shouts out, "Hoo ha!" but I have no idea what language that is.

I really like staying with Bubbie. Uncle Jack, Aunt Esther, and Buddy live in the apartment too, so I always have a good time there.

One Saturday morning Uncle Jack and I took Buddy out to the prairie that's close by, and while Uncle Jack looked on, I ran through the tall grasses with Buddy, and we played hide and seek. I did the hiding and he did the seeking. And no matter where I hid, he always found me.

In the afternoon Bubbie took me to the grocery store across the street and treated me to an Eskimo Pie. It was the first time I ever had one. An Eskimo Pie is just like an ice cream bar, only without the stick. You have to hold it with the wrapper. I wanted to share it with Bubbie, so in English I asked, "Would you like a bite, Bubbie?" And in Yiddish she answered, "Too much sugar for me." So I ate the whole thing. I ate it the way I eat all ice cream bars. First I scrape off that lovely chocolate coating with my teeth. Then I suck on the vanilla ice cream slowly, like I do on a Slo Poke.

Later in the day while Bubbie took a nap, I roamed around the apartment—an apartment that's almost like a garden, with pots of flowers, and plants with purple leaves on windowsills in every single room. And different flowered wallpaper in every room too, except for the kitchen and bathroom, which are painted white.

I studied the knickknacks and family photographs Bubbie has displayed on doily-covered tabletops. And on the wall above the couch—Bubbie calls it a davenport— are two huge brown oval frames with photos of Bubbie, and Zadie, my grandfather, who I never met because he died in Russia way before I was born. Bubbie, young and pretty, is wearing a dress with a high collar. And Zadie has a dark beard and is wearing a tall skullcap. Neither of them is smiling.

I heard click-clicking sounds on the wood floor and pretty soon Buddy trotted in. He seemed to know that nobody else was around, so he jumped up on the davenport, curled up, and went to sleep.

In the evening Aunt Esther had a date with a guy named George. I made myself comfortable on her bed and watched her get ready. I love watching her. I love watching her pin up her hair, put on makeup and jewelry, and dab Evening in Paris behind her ears. I watched as she put on red Hazel Bishop lipstick and matching nail polish, and applied extra rouge to her cheeks.

When Aunt Esther gets all dolled up she looks like the movie star Dorothy Lamour.

I followed her as she hummed and danced around the house searching for just the right thing to wear, changing from one outfit to another.

She slipped into a forest-green crepe dress, turned her back toward me and said, "Tell me the truth, Dorrie, does this dress make my tush stick out?"

I shrugged. "Only a little."

Off went the green crepe and on went a two-piece blue wool jersey.

"How about this one?"

"Much better," I told her.

She reached into the top drawer of her dresser and pulled out a brand-new, unopened box of Fanny Farmer chocolates.

"Here," she said. "A gift from my date. Enjoy yourself. And thank you for your help."

"Ooh, there's got to be at least two layers in here. How many pieces can I have?"

"As many as you want."

"Really? Don't you want any?"

"After the way that green dress looked on me I don't think I should be eating these."

After Aunt Esther left, I curled up on the davenport, listening to *The Life of Riley* on the radio, and wondering about her date with George. It must have been especially important for her. I never saw her so picky about what she wore. And why would George give her such a special box of chocolates?

I opened up the box and sure enough, there were two layers of chocolates. The fun thing about chocolates is that each one holds a secret. You never know what you'll find inside until you bite into it. I popped the first piece into my mouth just as Bubbie popped into the room with the unfinished sweater she was knitting for Uncle Jack.

"Ooh, a caramel," I announced, chewing happily. "This is so delicious." I held the box out to her. "Here, Bubbie, take a piece."

She shook her head and sat down next to me.

Then came the second piece. "Ah, a nut. My favorite."

"That's enough," said Bubbie. "Too much sugar for you."

"But all I had were two pieces," I told her.

"You had ice cream before."

"But that was in the afternoon. Now it's nighttime."

"It's too much for one day. You'll get sick."

Maybe Bubbie was right. I remembered the time I ate almost three boxes of Cracker Jack at a birthday party. And when I was finished, my stomach felt like it did the time I rode in an elevator in the Monadnock Building downtown. Every time the elevator operator stopped to let people on or off, my stomach dropped down to the floor.

So I closed up the box and put it away on a shelf behind me so I wouldn't be able to see it. And then I sat back down next to Bubbie and together we listened to the rest of *The Life of Riley*.

Early Sunday morning Bubbie and I were in the kitchen ready to do some baking. Even though my mother is a wonderful cook and baker, Bubbie is the best ever.

Bubbie doesn't even use recipes. I asked my mother about it once. "How can Bubbie cook and bake so well? She doesn't use recipes."

"She has a knack," my mother answered. "She goes by instinct. She goes by eye, by feel, and by taste."

But Bubbie does have one recipe that I know about. It's handwritten in Yiddish on a sheet of paper that she keeps at the bottom of a kitchen drawer. It's the recipe for my very favorite. A chocolate nut torte.

The torte is a cake made with ground hazelnuts and almonds and topped with whipped cream and strawberries. Bubbie knows how much I love it. She baked one for me this past June when I turned ten. And she was all set to make one for me that morning. That's when the idea hit me. I would bake a chocolate nut torte for Sweet Semester! I would watch Bubbie very closely and learn how to do it.

When Bubbie took the recipe from the drawer I could almost smell the bittersweet chocolate mingling with the vanilla flavoring that would be coming from the oven. I could almost taste the torte and see Bubbie smile and hear her shout, "Hoo ha!" when it came out—perfect as ever.

Right away my mouth started to water. So did Bubbie's eyes. She was looking at the recipe and crying.

I never saw anyone crying over a recipe before.

"Bubbie, are you okay?" I asked, looking into her eyes, the color of little blue cornflowers. My eyes are blue too. But there's more gray in them.

She nodded, wiped her eyes with a corner of her apron, and put the recipe back in the drawer. "Maybe later," she said. Then without a word, she went to the refrigerator and took out a small package wrapped in wax paper. She placed it on a dish that was clear and blue. You could see through it. Aunt Esther once

described the color as cobalt blue. Bubbie has a cupboard filled with dishes like that. Blue, pink, yellow, and green.

Aunt Esther and my mother got them for Bubbie a long time ago on "Dish Night" at the movies. A free dish for each ticket. They must've gone to a lot of movies back in the olden days to get all those dishes.

Bubbie also gave me a glass of milk and watched as I unwrapped the wax paper package to discover a beautiful chocolate cupcake covered with thick chocolate frosting. She knows that I am crazy about chocolate cupcakes.

"Oh Bubbie, thank you," I said. "What a terrific surprise!"

She answered me with a little smile and stayed with me for a few moments. And then it was my turn to watch her as she went across the hall to her bedroom, picked up her knitting, and sat down in her chair. But Bubbie didn't do any knitting. She just sat in her chair and stared into space. How could a recipe make her so sad?

Aunt Esther came into the kitchen as I finished up the cupcake.

"How was your date?" I asked her.

"Wonderful," she answered. "We had a lovely time." She poured herself some coffee and drank it standing up.

There were still lots of cake crumbs on the wrapper and I didn't want to miss any of it. So I stuck the wrapper in my mouth and began chewing.

"Delicious," I said.

"That's disgusting," said Aunt Esther. "Throw it away."

"But there's still lots of chocolate on it," I told her. "Please?"

She asked it like a question, but I knew it was an order. So I threw the wrapper in the garbage. What a waste.

But that cupcake wrapper gave me an idea. I couldn't wait to try it out.

CHAPTER SEVEN

Chocolate-Covered Gum

My father loves gum. So do I. Whenever I want a piece, all I have to do is reach into his jacket pockets and I am almost never disappointed. He keeps his pockets well supplied with Wrigley's Doublemint or Juicy Fruit. Juicy Fruit is my favorite.

Ever since the day when I disgusted Aunt Esther by chewing on the cupcake wrapper, I'd been wondering. How come there is no such thing as chocolate-covered gum? So I was thinking, maybe I could invent some. I could be like that lady, Ruth Wakefield, who invented chocolate chip cookies. Miss Fitzgerald told us about her when we were discussing inventors. I never thought chocolate chip cookies were invented. I thought inventions meant big ideas—like the telephone or electric lights. But then I found out that chocolate chip cookies were an invention too. So why couldn't I invent chocolate-covered gum? I would bring it in for Sweet Semester. It would be a big hit.

After school one day I went to Sunny's house to do homework. I was going to help her with spelling and she was going to help me with decimals. I'm always confused about where to put the decimal points.

I like to go to Sunny's house. Her mother works and we have the whole place to ourselves. The only thing is, we're not allowed in any room except Sunny's room or the kitchen—and only if we clean up after ourselves. The living room and dining room are kept in perfect order and are only used for company. I guess that's because Sunny's mother doesn't have much time to clean.

Before we ever got to the homework I had to tell Sunny my idea.

"Chocolate-covered gum."

"Chocolate-covered gum?" Sunny repeated.

"Yeah. I thought of it when I chewed on a cupcake wrapper."

Sunny looked up at the ceiling as if there was some-body up there who would tell her whether or not my idea was a good one.

"I think chocolate-covered gum would be swell. But why hasn't anyone invented it by now?"

"That's the whole idea behind inventions," I told her. "There are things that don't exist until someone comes along and invents it. We didn't have electric lights until Thomas Edison. Or the telephone until Alexander Graham Bell. Or chocolate chip cookies until Ruth Wakefield came along. So why should chocolate-covered gum be any different?"

"Makes sense," said Sunny.

I took a few pieces of Juicy Fruit gum out of my school bag and placed them on the table. Next, I took out the bag of chocolate chips my mother gave me when I told her that Sunny and I might do a little baking. I didn't tell her about the gum. I wanted her to be surprised.

Sunny snatched a pot from a cupboard and set it on the stove. "Okay," she said, "let's get this show on the road."

I was glad to see she was getting into the spirit of things. "If this comes out good we can bring it for Sweet Semester," I told her. "We can both go in on it because it will be spectacular."

Sunny began stirring the chocolate. "I can see it all now. Dorrie Meyers and Sunny Shapiro—inventors of chocolate-covered gum! We'll be famous. We'll be written up in all the newspapers in the country. Not just the *Chicago Daily News* and the *Tribune*."

"And maybe in *Betsy Belle*, too," I said. *Betsy Belle* is

filled with stories and comics and crafts—like how to make earmuffs. And there are articles about famous girls, like Margaret O'Brien. Sunny and I would probably be in an article about our chocolate-covered gum invention. Maybe Margaret O'Brien would even advertise a special kit that you could send away for to make the gum.

I unwrapped the sticks of Juicy Fruit and dropped them into the melted chocolate. "Get them nice and coated," I told Sunny. So she swirled the gum around with her spoon. She swirled and swirled. Then she looked deep into the pot and said, "Something's wrong. I can't find the gum. It disappeared."

I looked too. "Oh no! It melted!"

"What do we do now?" Sunny asked.

I tried to think of what Ruth Wakefield would do in a case like this. When it came to baking her cookies, she put chunks of chocolate in the batter thinking she was baking chocolate cookies. But the chocolate chunks never melted. And she ended up with chocolate chip cookies. The greatest cookies ever, by the way. A mistake that turned out for the best.

How could *our* mistake turn out for the best? I wondered. And then it came to me.

"Chocolate gum balls!" I cried out.

Sunny looked hopeful. And excited. With a spoon she

scooped the hot mixture out of the pot and onto a plate. And when it cooled off, we shaped the mixture into little balls and put them in her refrigerator to harden.

We worked on decimals and spelling for a whole half hour. But I still couldn't figure out those decimal points. Then we went to check on the gum balls. I could hardly wait to try one.

It was soft. There was no chew left to it.

"It tastes like candy," said Sunny.

"Yeah, candy we can't even eat."

At first I thought the whole afternoon was a waste. I didn't learn my decimals, Sunny didn't learn any spelling, and we didn't invent anything. But there was one thing I did learn.

I have no instinct.

Sunny and I spit out our invention into the garbage pail and cleaned up the kitchen so her mother wouldn't yell at us. Then I tucked my blouse into my skirt and went home.

How to Make Chocolate-Covered Gum

Don't even try it!

CHAPTER EIGHT

That Summer in New York

One day in October Miss Fitzgerald handed back our "What I Did on My Summer Vacation" compositions. She had them tacked up onto the bulletin board in the back of the room, and now she had to make space for pumpkins, witches, and coal-black cats.

I wonder why all teachers make us write those compositions. Why do they want to know what we did on our vacations? What if we didn't do anything? And why do they care?

For my composition I wrote about our trip to New York.

My father manufactures mattresses. And in the summer there was a mattress convention in New York City. I'm not sure what a mattress convention is, exactly, but I think it's a place where people get together to talk about mattresses and box springs. And maybe beds.

Both my father and mother thought it might be fun for all of us to go to New York for our vacation, because none of us had ever been there. And we hadn't gone on any real vacations in a long time. Mostly we've been taking short trips around Chicago, going to parks and museums and to the Garfield Park Conservatory.

So Artie packed the camera he received for his bar mitzvah and we hopped a train and went. I hope that someday I'll get to visit every one of the forty-eight states. So far, besides Illinois where I live, I've been to Wisconsin, Minnesota, and Indiana. And now I got to see New York.

There are lots of things to do and see in New York. And Artie took pictures of us visiting the Empire State Building, which is the tallest building in the world, and climbing the stairs to the top of the Statue of Liberty, right into the crown that Lady Liberty wears.

You have to take a ferryboat to the statue. And right before we got on, my father bought each of us a pack of chocolate-covered Brazil nuts. We ate the Brazil nuts on the boat. I've never tasted anything like them. They were so delicious. Chocolaty and crunchy. I would take a trip to New York anytime just to get them because I can't find any around here. So there we were, eating those scrumptious nuts on the blue

water and looking out at the statue.

"What a wonderful sight," my mother said, her eyes watering up. "Just think of all the immigrants who saw this very same statue when they came to America to start their new lives. How thrilling it must have been. If only our family in Europe could be so lucky. To be alive and to come here and see this too."

She wiped her eyes and put her arms around Artie and me. "I have always wanted to see the Statue of Liberty."

"Didn't you see it when you came here from Russia?" I asked her.

"I didn't come to New York. Neither did Daddy. Our boats sailed to Canada. My family took a train to Minneapolis and Daddy's family went to St. Paul."

"And Minneapolis is where you guys met. At a party, right?"

"The best party of my life," my father said, and he gave my mother's shoulder a little squeeze.

My father went on to tell us about *his* father who left Russia and went to St. Paul where he found work as a barrel maker. And when he saved enough money, he sent for my grandmother and their five children, including my father.

"My big dream was to come to America so I could wear pajamas to bed," my father said.

"Wearing pajamas was your big dream?" I asked.

"Where we lived in Russia there were many pogroms. Attacks on the Jews. Jews were murdered. Houses were burned. We ran into the forest to hide. So we always had to be dressed and ready to go."

"Oh, poor Daddy," I said, touching his hand.

I thought about how brave my father's family was to come to a strange new country, without knowing the language. And Bubbie, too. How did she bring six children here all by herself?

Immigrants must be very brave, I decided. And I tried to imagine being an immigrant. I would wear a babushka on my head, sail on a ship, and see the Statue of Liberty for the very first time, knowing I was in a free country where I could go to sleep in pajamas.

While we were in New York we stayed at a hotel and ate out at lots of restaurants because my mother couldn't make anything better and cheaper at home. And whenever we went out to eat, my father wore a smile like the one the cat wears in *Alice in Wonderland*.

I bought some scenic postcards and pasted a penny

stamp on each one to mail to Sunny during our trip. On each card I wrote, "Wish you were here because I miss you." And I really did.

One postcard showed an amusement park on Coney Island called Steeplechase. It pictured the Parachute Jump, which is a ride that starts high up in the sky before it drops down with a parachute billowing open, and which is a ride I didn't go on because it's probably a lot worse than an elevator ride in the Monadnock Building.

Another postcard showed the Automat on Times Square. It's an amazing cafeteria with a whole wall of little windows, with different food behind each one of them. You put nickels in a slot, open the door to the window, and take out whatever you want. We each opened our windows to cheese sandwiches on rye bread and chocolate cream pie.

Before we left New York I made another discovery. This time in a Brooklyn candy store. Chocolate egg creams. Egg creams are not made with eggs or cream. They're like chocolate phosphates only better. They have them all over New York. And they're deee-licious.

Artie took pictures of everything. And now whenever I look at them I remember, and will always remember,

New York with its restaurants, chocolate egg creams, chocolate-covered Brazil nuts, Empire State Building, Statue of Liberty, Steeplechase, and the Automat.

Can any other city be more exciting?

How to Make a Chocolate Egg Cream

INGREDIENTS
Get a tall glass.
Pour in:
  1 inch chocolate syrup
  1 inch milk
WHAT TO DO
Squirt in seltzer and stir until it gets white and foamy on the top.
(Stir from the bottom of the glass so you don't mess up the foam.)

CHAPTER NINE

We Hear About Victor

Even though I can't find those wonderful chocolate-covered Brazil nuts around here, I can buy plenty of chocolate candy bars at Ziffer's Drugstore. And sometimes I can get them for free at my Uncle Louie's grocery store.

Uncle Louie, who is my father's brother, owns a grocery store a short car ride away from where I live. Once in a while my mother and father take Artie and me there to visit him and also to give him some business.

When we went there on the evening of what I now call The Great Chocolate-Covered Gum Fiasco, my mother gave Artie and me the same short speech right before we entered the store.

"Remember—don't ask for anything, and if Uncle Louie offers you something, say 'no thank you'."

"Why do we have to say 'no thank you'?" I asked. "Why can't we just say 'yes'?"

"Because I don't want it to cost him anything whenever we come over."

"But why would it cost him anything? He owns the store. He's the boss."

Then Artie popped in with, "I don't think two five-cent candy bars will put him out of business."

"Never mind. Just do as I say."

Once we were inside, Uncle Louie asked, "Would you like something? Some candy, maybe?"

Yes, yes. A Hershey bar with almonds. Baby Ruth . . . Mounds . . . Chunky . . .

"No thank you, Uncle Louie."

But Uncle Louie insisted. "Go on, take something."

My Aunt Goldie was there helping out in the store. She said, "Take what you want. Don't be bashful."

I looked at my mother and waited for her go-ahead nod. And when it came, so did my big decision. Which candy bar to get? I choose a different bar every time I visit Uncle Louie's store. The last time I was there I asked for a Mounds bar because it's like getting two candy bars instead of just one. This time I chose a Baby Ruth, and Artie chose an Oh Henry! bar. My father helped himself to a pack of Juicy Fruit gum, and when Uncle Louie wasn't looking, he put a nickel on the counter.

Uncle Louie wasn't looking because he and my mother were talking about the missing relatives. That's all my family talked about lately. My mother, who usually never cared who answered the phone, now jumped to answer it every time it rang. And the mail—she usually took it out of the mailbox whenever she got around to it. Mostly Artie and I got to it first, on account of we're always sending away for something: secret compartment rings, decoders, pedometers. But now I kept finding the mailbox empty when I got home from school.

It was on a morning in November when my mother scared me half to death. I was standing in front of my bedroom mirror practicing how to cry. I was being Margaret O'Brien playing a war orphan. I pretended I had no home, no family. I was all alone, living in the ruins of a building in London, bombs falling all around me. I practiced being sad and scared, by making all kinds of weird faces. I tried to force tears to come. But none would. Maybe because I knew deep down I wasn't really a war orphan who was sad, scared, and alone.

I was in the middle of making one of those faces when Artie walked in. "What's wrong with you?" he asked. "You look like you just sucked on a lemon."

That's when we heard my mother scream.

Artie and I flew out of the bedroom and ran to her in the kitchen. She had a letter in her hand and she was crying. Really crying.

Now that's not unusual for my mother. She cries over the simplest things sometimes. She even cries over yellow daffodils because she says they're so sweet looking and beautiful.

I cried over roses once. But that's on account of I was smelling one in a bed of flowers and got stung by a bee.

But this time it was different. First my mother was crying and the next thing I knew she was laughing. And then she was crying again. She was hysterical. I worried that she was going mad, like Merle Oberon in the movie *Dark Waters*.

When she saw Artie and me standing there in shock, she threw herself at us, hugging us both and crying.

"What's going on?" Artie asked.

I was so scared I couldn't even open my mouth to say anything. I wanted my father to be home.

"Our Victor is alive," my mother said in between the laughing and crying. "I don't know about the others. But Victor is alive." She showed us the letter she received from a Jewish organization and read it out loud:

> *Dear Mrs. Meyers,*
> *We thank you for your inquiry concern-*
> *ing the Dubin families of Kovno, Lithuania.*
> *We were fortunate to locate Victor Dubin,*
> *son of Mina and Joseph Dubin. He is living*
> *in the Landsberg Displaced Persons Camp in*
> *Germany. He has inquired of you as well …*

When we finished the letter she ran to the phone and called Bubbie. She spoke in Yiddish, then in English, and then she was back to Yiddish. And she read the letter again.

After my mother hung up the phone, she went into the bedroom and closed the door.

Bubbie, Uncle Jack, and Aunt Esther came over right away. They wanted to see the letter for themselves.

My father, who was away doing errands, came home a little while afterward to find us sitting around the dining room table drinking coffee, tea, and milk (for Artie and me), and eating chocolate babka.

"Oh, a party," my father joked. "And I'm just in time."

My mother hurried to show him the letter too, and then everyone was talking a mile a minute. They talked about Victor and how grateful they were that he survived.

"Thank God, thank God."

They worried and wondered: about Victor's parents, Mina and Joseph; about Sophie, his grandmother and Bubbie's sister.

"What happened to them?"

"It can't be good."

"What did those Germans do?"

"That lousy Hitler!"

"This is a bitter time," Bubbie said, her eyes filling.

"But sweet, too," said my mother. "We have Victor."

We sat around the table, sad and happy at the same time. Bitter and sweet. It was like the first time I made hot cocoa. When I added the cocoa powder to hot milk, it tasted bitter and awful. But then I added sugar. And it all went down warm and sweet.

CHAPTER TEN

A Care Package for Victor

We decided to send a care package to Victor. My mother had already sent him a letter. She said, "He's been without for so long, it's the least we can do for him right now."

All of us were running around like chickens without heads getting the package ready.

Here's what went into the package:

Bubbie—the sweater she was knitting for Uncle Jack

Uncle Jack—socks and underwear

Aunt Esther—shirts that she bought at Mandel Brothers

Uncle Louie—a box of twenty-four Milky Ways

My mother—a big batch of chocolate chip

cookies (She wanted to send him the carrot cake she's famous for, but thought it would arrive stale.)

My father—ten packs of Juicy Fruit—and money, which will be from both him and my mother

Artie—a brand new genuine brown leather wallet (He received four of them for his bar mitzvah.)

As for me—I had no idea!

But time was running out and I wanted to send something too. Finally I had an idea. And here's how I came up with it: I'd been thinking about Victor, wondering what he looked like. So I figured Victor would probably be wondering about us, too.

I went into the dining room and looked through the drawer where we keep our pictures. There were so many of them. But I picked out a few snapshots that I liked.

One showed my mother, father, Artie, and me taken on a Sunday afternoon at Garfield Park this summer. We are all standing together. My mother is wearing a flower in her hair. Her arm is around Artie's shoulder, and my father's arm is linked through mine. I am squinting in the sun.

There was one of Bubbie sitting on a bench in the park, with Uncle Jack and Aunt Esther standing behind her.

I also found a picture of Artie and me in the alley next to our apartment building. Buddy is sitting in front of us and I am holding his leash.

With these pictures, Victor wouldn't have to wonder about us. He'd know what we look like. His American family.

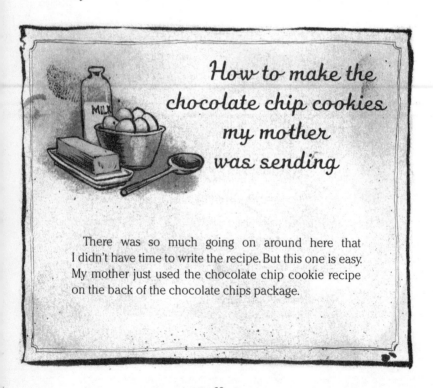

How to make the chocolate chip cookies my mother was sending

There was so much going on around here that I didn't have time to write the recipe. But this one is easy. My mother just used the chocolate chip cookie recipe on the back of the chocolate chips package.

CHAPTER ELEVEN

Thanksgiving and Aunt Jenny

I love Thanksgiving! I love when it's cold and gray and drizzly outside and we spend the day at Bubbie's house, where it's warm and cozy, all of us together, eating turkey with the works.

Earlier in the day my mother and father went to Uncle Louie's grocery store to do some last-minute shopping. He was keeping the store open for half a day, and my mother needed some items for a few of the side dishes and desserts she was bringing to Bubbie's.

I got to thinking about my mother and how busy she always is, with all the shopping and cooking and cleaning she does. And how especially busy she was getting Victor's care package together. So I decided to surprise her. I would contribute to the Thanksgiving dinner with a dessert of my own. And I knew exactly what I would bake. Brownies.

I've watched my mother bake brownies lots of times. It seemed easy enough. And I would use her easy, can't-miss recipe. I figured that if I baked the brownies, she wouldn't have to do any baking at all. And if they came out good, and I couldn't think of anything more original, I could even bake brownies for Sweet Semester.

First I gathered up the supplies and ingredients and preheated the oven. Then I put on one of my mother's aprons, turned on the radio in the dining room to keep me company, and got to work.

I melted the Spry and chocolate baking squares in a pot over a low fire, just like my mother does. But unlike my mother, who mixes all the ingredients in the pot, I decided to use her Mixmaster. It would be faster and easier. That way my arm wouldn't get tired from mixing so much.

When the Spry and the chocolate were melted, I set it aside and cracked the eggs into the bowl of the Mixmaster. Then I fished out the eggshells and added the sugar and vanilla. The kitchen was humming with the sound of the motor and my singing of "Oh What a Beautiful Morning." This was so easy. *Why didn't my mother make brownies this way?* I wondered.

With the beaters still going at high speed, I added the mixture of flour and baking soda. And *poof!* Flour explosion!

All over the kitchen! All over me! I turned off the motor, and when the fog settled, I added more flour to make up for the flour that had escaped. But how much? I didn't know, so I guessed. I turned the motor on low and continued. I mixed and I sang. I couldn't believe how smooth and creamy the batter was becoming. I was Betsy in the Kitchen.

I poured the batter into a greased baking pan and stuck it in the oven. While the brownies were baking, I cleaned up the mess I made. I even washed and dried the breakfast dishes my mother left in the sink because she was in such a hurry to get to Uncle Louie's.

The aroma in the kitchen was warm and wonderful. Just like it is when my mother bakes. And now for the best part: I saved the mixing bowl for last. I scraped off whatever batter I could from inside the bowl and licked off the spoon. The batter was so good I could only imagine how the brownies would taste.

So there I was, scraping and licking, when Artie walked in.

"Jeepers, you look like a cake," he said.

"Want some? There's a whole other side I didn't touch."

He grabbed me by the hand and pulled me into the dining room. "Come on. *Aunt Jenny's Real Life Stories* is on the radio."

"What do I care? I hate those soap operas."

"Just listen. Aunt Jenny will help you become a better cook. She'll help you with Spry."

"Oh sure. A shortening will help me become a better cook. You shouldn't believe all those commercials."

I sat down on the couch and listened to Aunt Jenny of Littleton, U.S.A. talking about finding true happiness.

Pretty soon the commercial came on and now Aunt Jenny was telling how Spry could help any cook, "from butterfingers to expert," become a better cook. That's when I heard the key in the front door and my father asking, "What's burning?"

"Oh no!" I cried. "It can't be!"

We all ran into the smoke-filled kitchen. My mother grabbed a potholder and pulled out a pan of black cement. She set it in the sink. My eyes were tearing from the smoke. Everyone else's eyes were tearing too.

"Oh, my beautiful brownies," I sobbed. "It's all Aunt Jenny's fault. Her and her Spry. And I wasted a whole cup of sugar."

"Aw, honey," my mother said, wrapping her arms around me.

I burrowed my head into her skunk coat, which Artie and I both think smells like a skunk when it gets wet.

"I will never be an expert," I cried. "I will always be butterfingers."

I cried and cried and couldn't stop.

How to Make My Mother's Can't-Miss Chocolate Brownies

Okay, so I *did* miss with these brownies. Here is the right way to make them.

INGREDIENTS

1/2 cup unsalted butter or vegetable shortening
2 squares unsweetened baking chocolate
1 cup sugar
3 eggs

1 teaspoon vanilla
1/2 cup flour
1/2 teaspoon baking powder
1 cup chopped walnuts
1/4 cup chocolate chips

WHAT TO DO

Preheat oven to 350°.

Lightly grease an 8- or 9-inch square baking pan.

Melt butter and chocolate squares in medium saucepan over low heat. Remove from heat.

Add sugar, eggs, vanilla, flour, and baking powder and stir until well blended.

Stir in walnuts and chocolate chips.

Pour batter into pan.

(You can sprinkle extra walnuts and chocolate chips on top if you want.)

Bake 30-35 minutes. Let cool and cut into squares.

Hint: Don't get caught up in a radio program while you're waiting for the brownies to get done.

CHAPTER TWELVE

Bubbie and I Cook and Bake for Hanukkah

Hanukkah came early in December and Bubbie was cooking and baking up a storm for our Hanukkah dinner. The whole house already smelled wonderful from the potato latkes she was frying up. She wanted me to come over earlier so she could show me how to bake mandel bread. Mandel bread isn't really bread. It's a cookie. Bubbie loves to bake it. And in my honor she was going to make it chocolate.

"I have no instinct for baking," I told her. "I'm waiting for cake mixes to come out."

"What is a cake mix?" Bubbie asked in Yiddish, as she cracked a few eggs into a bowl.

"I read in one of Ma's magazines—*Ladies' Home Journal* or *Good Housekeeping*—that they're experimenting with cake mixes. Almost everything you need will come in a box and all you have to do is add water and eggs."

I waited for Bubbie to say, "Hoo ha!" But she wrinkled up her nose. "Cake from a box? *Feh!*"

She gathered up flour, cocoa, sugar, oil, and set them on the table.

"See, for mandel bread we do not need a box," she said.

As she measured and mixed, baking by eye, by taste, by instinct, I created a recipe. I wrote down the amounts of everything she used, wrote down everything she did. I helped her roll the dough into logs, bake them, slice them, and bake them again.

"How come you and Ma both have magic hands, while I'm a klutz in the kitchen?" I asked.

Bubbie laughed. "When your mother was growing up she made plenty of mistakes. She used yeast that didn't rise. She got mixed up between baking soda and baking powder. One time—and this is a secret—she was baking mandel bread like we are now. But instead of adding sugar, she added salt. A whole cup of salt."

"Oh no!" I said scrunching up my face. "It must've tasted awful."

"Believe me. It was worse than awful. But she prac-ticed. And you see? She learned. In time you will learn too. Don't worry."

"What about you, Bubbie. When did you learn?"

"When I was very young I was already helping my mother in the kitchen. We baked and sold bread and cakes to make a living. "

Looking at Bubbie's sweet, wrinkled face, it was hard to imagine her ever being young—even though I always see that picture of her in the oval frame. I was glad I came earlier to be with her. And before Aunt Esther and Uncle Jack came home from work we even got to sample the mandel bread, and the latkes that I slathered with sour cream. They were both wonderful.

Later my mother and father and Artie joined us and we all gathered at the front room window to light the Hanukkah menorah. At my house on Hanukkah we light candles. Pretty little orange candles. But here at Bubbie's we use the menorah she brought to America all the way from Russia. Instead of candles it uses oil.

Bubbie poured olive oil into the tiny cups and floated a wick in each cup. And then my father was given the honor of lighting the wicks and saying the blessings.

So now our menorah joined all the others in the windows of apartment buildings up and down the street.

After dinner, before we left, Uncle Jack reached into his pocket and pulled out two shiny silver dollars.

"Hanukkah gelt," he said to Artie and me. And he pressed the coins into our hands. This dollar will go to the food fund, I decided.

It was a wonderful day. And I was glad I came early to spend it with Bubbie. She gave me hope. Maybe I'll have magic hands too, someday. But just in case that doesn't happen, at least I'll have her recipe. And there's one thing I'm sure of. I won't ever forget the Hanukkah when I came to bake mandel bread with Bubbie.

How to Make Bubbie's Chocolate Mandel Bread

INGREDIENTS

1/3 cup vegetable oil
3/4 cup sugar
2 eggs
1 teaspoon vanilla extract
1 teaspoon almond extract
1/4 cup cocoa

1-3/4 cups flour
1-1/2 teaspoons baking powder
grated orange peel from 1 orange
2 tablespoons orange juice
2/3 cup chopped walnuts

WHAT TO DO

Preheat oven to 350°.

Lightly grease a cookie sheet.

Stir flour, cocoa, and baking powder together in a bowl and set aside.

In a large bowl mix oil, sugar, eggs, vanilla and almond extracts.

Gradually stir in flour and cocoa mixture.

Add grated orange peel, orange juice, and walnuts.

Chill batter for 30 minutes.

Divide dough into 4 equal parts, and roll each part into a 6-inch log.

Flatten logs to make them about 2 inches wide.

Place logs on cookie sheet (with space in between each log).

Bake for 30 minutes.

Let cool, and cut into diagonal slices about 3/4 inch wide.

(Bubbie puts the slices back in the oven for a few minutes to get them toasty. But I can't wait that long, so I eat them right after she cuts them. Yum!)

Nut Cluster Disaster

On a December day, while we were cutting out snow-flake designs to tape onto the windows next to our paper snowmen, Miss Fitzgerald walked up to the front of the room and asked, "What do you think about having a holiday party on Friday before school lets out for winter vacation?"

Cheers and whistles went up from the class. I would've whistled too, but I don't know how.

Anyway, I love parties in school. One reason is that they're fun. The other reason is that you don't have to do any work.

"What shall we have for refreshments?" she asked. "Who wants to bring what?"

There were all kinds of suggestions.

"Candy."

"Potato chips."

"Pop."

"Chocolate cupcakes." That was me. And I went on to volunteer my mother to bake cupcakes for the whole class, including Miss Fitzgerald.

As soon as I offered my mother, I knew I had made a BIG mistake. Here's why.

Last year Artie volunteered to take the classroom curtains home during summer vacation so my mother could wash and iron them. My mother was not too happy.

"Thank you for volunteering me," she said to Artie. "As if I don't have enough work to do. I wish you would have asked me first."

So now when I was walking home from school with Sunny, I told her about Artie and the curtains. "I'd better bake the cupcakes myself. I don't know if my mother would appreciate being volunteered again. And besides, I'll be needing her help for Sweet Semester."

"That's okay," said Sunny, who volunteered to bring licorice. "I'll help you. I just hope we have better luck this time."

"No chocolate-covered gum," I told her.

"No chocolate gum," she said, laughing.

"Do you know what you're making yet for Sweet Semester?" I asked. "It's coming up pretty soon and I'm getting nervous."

"Well actually, I do have an idea. If you don't mind, that is. I got the idea from your brother."

"You got an idea from Artie?"

"Yeah. From Artie and his marshmallow snowman. I thought I'd make s'mores. They're easy. And everybody likes them. And I still have to figure out something meaningful to write in my essay. But you can make them instead if you want to. After all, Artie's your brother."

Like my mother said, Sunny really is a person of fine character. "No, you go ahead. It's your idea," I told her. "I'll think of something. Right now I have enough to worry about with the cupcakes."

But guess what? I didn't have to worry about baking cupcakes after all. I found something I thought would be much better. And here's how.

When I came home from school that day, the latest issue of *Betsy Belle* was waiting for me on the dining room table. In this issue, in "Betsy in the Kitchen," Betsy and one of her friends from the Betsy Belle Club were making chocolate nut clusters. The recipe looked so easy. And you just know how wonderful something with chocolate, nuts, and raisins would have to taste. Probably just like a Chunky. I called Sunny right away to tell her. And we planned for her to come over on Thursday so we could make the nut clusters together.

Nut clusters are much more original than cupcakes. And easier, too. Cupcakes can be tricky. Lots of things can go wrong. You can bake them too long or not long enough. Or they could fall in the pan and sink in the middle. I know this is true because when my mother bakes a cake she always tells Artie and me not to jump around in the kitchen or the cake will fall.

But with chocolate nut clusters, what could happen?

When Sunny came over, we had the kitchen to ourselves. Artie was away playing basketball at the JPI (that stands for "Jewish People's Institute") and my mother was out shopping. But she left us everything that we would need.

"Let's pretend I'm Betsy and you're a member of the Betsy Belle Club," I told Sunny.

"I'll be Patti," said Sunny.

We had the recipe and directions spread out in front of us. Here's what it said:

Chocolate Nut Clusters

2 cups chocolate chips
1 tablespoon unsalted butter or vegetable shortening
1/2 cup raisins
1/2 cup nuts

In a double boiler, melt the chocolate chips and butter or vegetable shortening until smooth.
Remove from heat.
Stir in raisins and nuts.
Drop by tablespoons onto wax paper.
Let cool.

"These nut clusters are simple to make," I told my invisible audience. "It shouldn't take long to do this."

"Right you are, Betsy. I'll fill the bottom part of the double boiler with water while you measure the ingredients."

"Thank you, Patti. Now we'll boil the water. Then we'll pour the chocolate chips into the top part of the pot and add the butter."

"Oooh, Betsy, look how nicely it melts. Now we can add the raisins and nuts."

"How lucky we are, Patti, that Mother chopped up all these walnuts for us."

"And won't Mother be surprised when she sees how wonderful they came out?"

Suddenly I stopped being Betsy and told Sunny, "I think we might have a problem. What if this isn't enough for the whole class? What if the kids want seconds? Or Miss Fitzgerald wants to give some to the teachers because they taste so good? She might even want to give a few to the principal. We need more chocolate. And I don't think we have any more in the house."

"Let me look around and see if I can find some," said Sunny as I continued stirring. And she searched all over the kitchen.

"Hurry, before it gets too thick!" I told her.

"I found some!" she cried out. "Lots!" And she handed me some chocolate squares wrapped in wax paper.

"Great!" We added the squares to the mixture, and when everything was melted nice and smooth, we dropped spoonfuls of the mixture onto pans covered with wax paper, and placed them in the Frigidaire to cool.

While we waited, we looked through *Betsy Belle*, trying to decide which fashions we liked and which ones we didn't. Most of the dresses were frilly and had puffed sleeves.

"I hate frills and puffs," I told Sunny.

"So do I," she said. "Too fancy."

I pointed out that most of the girls had ribbons tied around their braids. Personally I am not a fan of ribbons in my hair.

In this issue, Margaret O'Brien was advertising her Candy Kitchen again. Sunny and I thought we might send away for it some day.

When it seemed like the clusters were cool, we pulled the pans out of the Frigidaire. They were beautiful.

"Look, Sunny, they're just like the ones in the magazine. And at the candy counter in Woolworth's." Maybe Bubbie was right about practice.

"Let's sample it," she said. "Just to make sure they taste good."

"We'd better not," I told her. "We need to make sure there's enough for everyone. These are going to be a major hit."

We were all having a great time at the party the next day, singing songs like "Frosty the Snowman" and "Jingle Bells," and eating popcorn and potato chips, and Sunny's licorice, and the nut clusters. The kids liked them so much

I considered making them for Sweet Semester.

But after a while I wasn't feeling too good and I found myself running back and forth to the bathroom. So did Sunny. So did some of the other kids. Soon the whole class was running to the bathroom. Miss Fitzgerald left the room too, but I didn't know where she went.

By the time I got home I was feeling better. And when I told my mother what happened, she said, "It sounds like a touch of food poisoning."

But later that evening my mother asked my father and Artie and me, "Did anyone see my laxative? I had the chocolate Ex-Lax wrapped in wax paper near the sink and forgot to put it back in the medicine cabinet. Now I can't find it."

Uh-oh.

I wish *Betsy Belle* had gotten lost in the mail.

CHAPTER FOURTEEN

Happy New Year, 1946

It wasn't a very happy new year for Uncle Louie. He was going out of business. He and Aunt Goldie came over on New Year's Day to tell my mother and father about it.

"I knew this would happen," he said over tea and carrot cake. "I saw it coming."

Artie and I were lying on the floor in the front room playing Monopoly and listening.

"I hope this has nothing to do with those candy bars we've been getting from him," I whispered.

"Dorrie, don't be stupid. Uncle Louie is going out of business because a new A&P opened up a couple of blocks away from his store."

"That's so sad for him," I said.

"And it's sad for us too. There go our free candy bars."

"What chance does the little guy have over a behemoth supermarket?" Uncle Louie went on.

"Maybe it's for the best," said Aunt Goldie.

"How could it be for the best? We'll be headed for the poorhouse."

"Something will turn up," I heard my mother say.

"You can always go into the mattress business with me," my father told him.

At that point the phone rang and I got up to answer it. Aunt Esther was on the line and we started to talk.

"What?" I shouted. "That's wonderful! I can't believe it!"

"Who is it? What's wonderful? What can't you believe?" my mother called out.

"Aunt Esther is engaged!" I announced to everyone. "George proposed last night at a New Year's Eve party!"

Now they were all shouting too. "Mazel tov! Mazel tov!" and they came running over to the phone. But I kept on talking.

"When's the wedding? Really? You want *me*?"

Then I made my second announcement. "They're getting married in June and Aunt Esther wants me to be a junior bridesmaid!" That's when my mother practically grabbed the phone away from me so she could talk.

Even though the news about Aunt Esther was good,

when my mother got off the phone she told us something that was not so good.

"They'll be moving to Minneapolis," she said.

"Minneapolis? Why?" I asked. "Why don't they just stay here?"

"That's where George lives. He teaches school there. And Esther said that he loves Minnesota."

"I heard that Minnesota has ten thousand lakes," I told Artie later.

"That's probably because they count every puddle as a lake," said Artie.

I had a lake in my nose a few days later. I came down with my first cold and fever of the year and had to stay home from school. One of the worst things about being sick is having to drink the most disgusting concoction you can imagine. A guggle muggle.

A guggle muggle is made with egg yolks, sugar, and hot milk. And whenever I get a cold, I get a guggle muggle.

One night when I couldn't sleep because I was having a coughing fit, a dark figure appeared in my room and turned on the light. It was my mother in her nightgown. And in her hand was ... oh, no! The dreaded guggle muggle! I hid under the covers but she pulled them away.

"Here, drink this. You'll feel better."

I was coughing violently and shaking my head.

"Just a little. You don't have to finish it."

I kept shaking my head, which made my mother disappear. But soon she was back again, this time with the same guggle muggle in disguise. She had mixed cocoa into it.

"Here. It's a nice hot chocolate drink. You won't even taste the eggs. Try it."

So I tried it. And there was nothing nice about it. It was still disgusting.

There are some things even chocolate can't fix.

The next morning my mother tried to disguise the oatmeal with cocoa too. I just can't eat oatmeal—or any cooked cereal, chocolate or not. So I sat at the table and let the spoon play with the cereal.

"You know," my mother said, "the children in Europe are so hungry they would give anything for that cereal."

"I know," I answered. "That's why we're donating to the food fund. And I really wish I could give them my cereal, too."

She sat down across from me with a cup of coffee. Mostly she just makes coffee. I hardly ever see her drink it. She pours herself about half a cup and lets it cool. And then she doesn't drink it because it's not hot enough. So she saves it and reheats it later in the day and does the same thing all over again.

"Ma," I said as I was fishing around in my bowl, "I really need your help. Sweet Semester is almost here. And everybody but me knows what they're bringing." I thought about having Bubbie help me with the chocolate torte. But I didn't want her to cry over the recipe again.

"Oh, Dorrie, I can't think right now. But since I have to bake something for Artie's graduation, we can think of something for you then too."

She fiddled with the salt and pepper shakers. "All I can think about is trying to make arrangements to bring Victor here. We don't want him to stay in that DP camp any longer than he has to."

I know that DP stands for displaced persons. The camp is for people who were made homeless by the war. They live there until they can find a place to go.

"So he's all alone," I said. I couldn't imagine being all alone. Being the only one left in my family.

"He's alone *now*," my mother said, getting up to bring her cup over to the sink. "But not for long. Soon he'll have a whole new family—with all of us." I heard my mother's voice tremble, and even though her back was toward me I knew she was crying.

After a while she sat back down at the table and explained that because we have a small apartment, Victor would live with Bubbie and Uncle Jack and Buddy. And now that Aunt Esther was getting married, he would have a room of his own. We would see each other all the time, though, because our apartments are so close to each other.

This was very good news. For Victor and for me.

But there was other news. "Aunt Esther and George won't be leaving for Minneapolis until the end of August. They have to wait for their house to be fixed up. And they expect it to be ready before George starts teaching in September. In the meantime they'll stay at Bubbie's."

"But what about Victor? Where will he stay until they leave?"

"He'll stay here for a while. With us."

"Oh. In the dining room? On the sofa bed?" It would be so much fun to have him here, I thought. Sort of like having another brother.

"No, Dorrie. I think he should stay in your room. With Artie."

"My room? But what about me?"

"You'll be on the sofa. It'll just be for a short time. Victor hasn't had a home for so long. He deserves a room of his own. Or almost his own."

I knew my mother was right. That he needed the room more than I did. But still, I had my own little corner of that room. With my powder blue chintz bedspread and my collection of tiny glass animals on my dresser and my Dixie cup lids with movie star photos on the back and my marbles and the giant stuffed panda my father brought me from a trip to Canada. I really didn't want to give up my corner. I love my corner.

When I was well enough to go back to school, Miss Fitzgerald greeted me with a smile. "I'm glad you're back, Dorrie." And then she addressed the class. She had big news.

"As you know, the end of the first semester is approaching. Ordinarily you would be moving on to the second semester, Five-A, with a new teacher in a new classroom. But I've just received word that I will be teaching you in Five-A too. We will be together until the end of June."

The whole room rang with cheers and whistles. Miss Fitzgerald is a teacher that all kids like. I would be happy to have her for a teacher until I graduated from eighth grade.

"Because of this," she continued, "you have until June to prepare for Sweet Semester."

The cheers and whistles turned to moans and groans.

"Nuts!" said Freddie Bass.

"Phooey!" said Estelle Goodman. "That's so far away."

Far away was right. Now I'd have to wait five whole months to meet the reporter and photographer from the *Chicago Daily News*.

"Think of it this way," said Miss Fitzgerald. "By June you'll have that much more time to save up money for our food fund."

Well, that was one good thing all right. And the next good thing was that I would have more time to think of something to make. Maybe I would have a Sweet Semester after all.

How to Make a Guggle Muggle

You don't want to know!

CHAPTER FIFTEEN

I Slip and Artie Graduates

At the end of January we celebrated Artie's graduation from Lawson Elementary School. Artie was valedictorian of his class, so he was going to give a speech on the stage in front of the whole assembly hall.

I can't imagine giving a speech to so many people. I'd be so nervous. I hope I'm not valedictorian of my class. But I guess there's no chance of that on account of my problems with decimals.

Artie was walking around the house practicing his speech on behalf of the class of January 1946, bidding everyone welcome to their graduation exercises and thanking parents, teachers, and the principal for everything they'd done in preparing the students to become good citizens of the future.

Sometimes Artie acted goofy and started his speech

with "Friends, Romans, countrymen," which I think is from Shakespeare.

On the day of the graduation the family was invited to come over in the afternoon after the ceremony for a reception. My mother had planned on baking "Aunt Jenny's Chocolate Rapture Cake" in the morning.

"I have wanted to try this recipe ever since I saw it in the book I ordered from Aunt Jenny's radio program," she said as she gathered the ingredients. "I just love the name."

I was going to help her and maybe learn something, too. And I just knew that nothing would go wrong because we'd be doing everything together. And we'd be using Spry. By this time I had already forgiven Aunt Jenny and Spry for the brownie episode on Thanksgiving.

Well, something did go wrong. I slipped on the Spry.

How was I to know that a glob of Spry would fall on the floor and that I would step into it? How was I to know that I would fall on the floor too, and bang my finger against the cupboard and spend the morning at the doctor's office where I learned that my swollen finger was just sprained and not broken and I could go home just in time for Artie's graduation but not in time for "Aunt Jenny's Chocolate Rapture Cake"?

Luckily we were not without cake for the reception. Kaplan's Bakery saved the day. I went there with my mother, and it's a good thing, too. She chose a couple of boring coffee cakes, but I picked out a double chocolate layer cake topped with a cherry.

Artie received some presents from relatives who seemed to have forgotten what they gave him for his bar mitzvah. More wallets and fountain pens.

The day after the graduation Artie generously gave me one of the pens. A blue Esterbrook. For keeps.

"Oh, Artie, thank you. It's just what I needed. The pen I have leaks like crazy."

"I know," he said. "Maybe now you can get rid of those perpetual ink stains on your fingers."

"I'm going to start using this right now."

I already knew what I would be writing. A letter to Margaret O'Brien. I wanted to ask her how she played such a believable part as a war orphan in *Journey for Margaret*.

I filled up my pen with sky blue ink, and went searching for just the right stationery. It had to be something special. Something fancy. She was, after all, a movie star.

In a dining room cabinet there was a drawer filled with all kinds of stationery. Mostly ugly. But there was some interesting hotel stationery from places my father stayed at when he went to different cities for conventions. I also found some sheets of stationery from the Belden-Stratford Hotel right here in Chicago. My parents stayed there one weekend a few years ago. An anniversary gift from some relatives. My mother said it was okay to use a sheet.

So with my new Esterbrook and my Belden-Stratford stationery, I sat down and wrote:

Dear Margaret O'Brien,

I read about you all the time in my Betsy Belle *magazines. And I have seen all of your movies. You make each role you play so believable.*

A long time ago I saw you in Journey for Margaret *and I never forgot it. You were so real as a war orphan. How were you able to make yourself cry?*

In June my class is having something called Sweet Semester. We'll be collecting money to send to hungry children and children who became real orphans because of the war. We're supposed to bring in a dessert that we've made by ourselves and write an essay about why we made it. Then the class

*votes and the winners will be written up in
the* Chicago Daily News. *Our pictures will be
in there too.*

*I have no idea what I'm going to make
yet. So I don't know what I'm going to write
in my essay. I hope I won't get nervous reading it in front of an audience.*

*Please answer me if you can. Thank you
and keep up the good work!*

Your fan,

Dorrie Meyers

P.S. What's it like to be famous?

I enclosed the letter in a Belden-Stratford envelope,
pasted on a three-cent stamp, and addressed the envelope
to Margaret O'Brien in care of *Betsy Belle* on Vanderbilt
Avenue in New York City.

Probably Margaret wouldn't even answer my letter.
But it would be fun if she did.

Anyway, because of Artie, I got myself a brand-new
fountain pen.

Here is the "Chocolate Rapture Cake"—the one we never
got around to making. So I don't know how it tastes.

Chocolate Rapture Cake

Oven temperature: 350°

Baking time: 25-30 minutes

Yield: 2 round 9-inch layers

Sift 1-3/4 cups **flour**, 1-1/2 cups **sugar**, 3/4 teaspoon **salt**, 1/2 teaspoon **baking powder**, 3/4 teaspoon **baking soda** into mixing bowl.

Add 1/2 cup **vegetable shortening**, 3 melted **chocolate baking squares**, 1 cup **buttermilk**, 1 teaspoon **vanilla**.

Beat 200 strokes (2 minutes by hand or on mixer at low speed).

Add 2 unbeaten **eggs**.

Beat 200 strokes (same as above).

Stir in 1 cup shredded **coconut**.

Pour into two lightly coated 9-inch round cake pans.

Bake until toothpick comes out clean.

Cool and remove from pans.

Spread with **whipped cream** frosting between layers and on top and sides.

Dribble melted and cooled mixture of 1/2 ounce **bittersweet chocolate** and 1/2 teaspoon **vegetable shortening** around rim of cake.

CHAPTER SIXTEEN

Getting Ready for Victor

By the middle of March it was all arranged for Victor to be coming to America in a couple of months. My mother kept saying how he's one of the lucky ones. "He has family to come home to," she said.

And then our whole apartment was turned upside down. My father had all of us help move the furniture out of the bedroom so he could give the walls a fresh coat of paint. My mother washed and starched the curtains and started to work on a new bedspread for him. A navy blue chenille. "He shouldn't have to sleep on a bed with a powder blue chintz spread," she said.

"He won't care," I said. "It's just for a couple of months. It *is* just for a couple of months, isn't it?" I was acting like a spoiled brat. I knew it and my mother knew it. I recognized that look of disappointment on her face. I can always recognize it. She purses her lips together and looks at me sideways.

"Dorrie, after all Victor has been through I hope you won't begrudge him a nice place to sleep."

"What's 'begrudge'?" I asked.

"It means that you're unwilling to give him something that he needs."

"I'm willing," I said. "Sort of."

Also in March we bought tons of groceries at Uncle Louie's going-out-of-business sale. I think we bought too many apples.

"We have to eat them up before they go bad," my mother told us.

So I used some of them for ... guess what! Chocolate caramel apples. And you know something? They came out GREAT! And there were no mishaps. No burning, no slipping on Spry, and nobody had to run to the bathroom. Hoo ha! Finally, something for Sweet Semester.

One day in April Miss Fitzgerald walked up to the front of the room and said, "Class, we have a little more than two months to go before Sweet Semester. How many of you have now come to a decision about what you're making?" And this time most of the hands shot up. Including Sunny's. Including mine! And voices rang out throughout the room.

"I'm making brownies!"

"Cheesecake!"

"Fig newtons!"

"I'm going to make taffy apples!" Estelle Goodman blurted out.

What? Estelle Goodman was going to make taffy apples? That's practically the same as caramel apples. Now what was I supposed to make? I had nothing. Zero! It wasn't fair.

"Let's not give our ideas away," Miss Fitzgerald said. "We want everything to be a surprise."

This was a surprise, all right. To me. And to Sunny, too.

"Maybe this is for the best," she whispered to me from across the aisle. "You'll think of something even better."

"You sound like my Aunt Goldie," I whispered back.

A few minutes later Sunny passed me a note. "You can make those nut clusters. Only this time you'll just use real chocolate."

And I wrote back: "They'll remind everyone of the party when they got sick."

Miss Fitzgerald told us to tell our parents to save the date, and to remember about the food fund.

"June is just around the corner, class," she said. "We'll have lots of work to do before then. We'll have to clean up this room and make it spick-and-span for our guests."

I thought about my mother and Bubbie coming. And all the guests, too. Everybody would be there to taste the desserts. To see who wins. The whole city of Chicago would read about us in the paper. I had to come up with something special. I just had to.

Even though I wasn't going to make chocolate caramel apples for Sweet Semester, here's the recipe I used with the apples we bought up at Uncle Louie's grocery store.

How to Make Chocolate Caramel Apples

INGREDIENTS
6 apples and 6 Popsicle sticks
1 package chocolate caramels
(14 oz.)

1/2 cup chopped nuts (if you like nuts)

WHAT TO DO
Insert Popsicle sticks into stem end of apples.
Place caramels in a saucepan on low heat. Stir until melted.
Dip apples into caramel until completely coated.
Pour chopped nuts onto wax paper and roll apples to cover.
Place apples on wax paper and wait 15 minutes until firm.
Store in refrigerator.

CHAPTER SEVENTEEN

A Blue Dress with Puffy Sleeves

Aunt Esther was going to have a blue wedding.

My mother was anxious to get started on my dress. "We should at least buy the patterns and fabric," she said.

My mother sews her own clothes. Mine too. Mostly I don't mind it, but I'd like to get store-bought clothes once in a while. Sunny is lucky. Her mother can't sew. So she gets to buy her clothes at all kinds of fun stores.

I'm lucky my mother doesn't make shoes. At least I get to buy those in a shoe store. I love to try on shoes and stand at the X-ray machine and look through a viewer and watch as I wiggle my toes. That's how you see if the shoes fit right and your toes aren't all scrunched together without any room to grow.

My father and Artie are lucky too. They get to buy their clothes in stores all the time. My mother once made Artie a shirt, but he never wore it.

There are two things that I don't like about getting my clothes made. First I have to go with my mother to Sears Roebuck to look at patterns and fabrics. Then every time I get fitted I have to stand real straight and still while she measures and pins. And every part of me itches and sometimes I get stuck with one of the pins.

Today my mother picked me up after school and we headed right toward Sears.

"Can we stop somewhere for a grilled cheese sandwich and a malt or chocolate milk before we start looking? I'm hungry."

I remembered the time my mother once took me to the lunch counter at Woolworth's. It was right after a doctor's appointment. The nurse drew some blood from me and I almost fainted away. She woke me up with some smelling salts, but I was still woozy. On the way home we stopped at Woolworth's and my mother bought me grilled cheese and a tall glass of chocolate milk. I really felt better after that. I was hoping she'd do the same thing today, because I always feel like fainting when I look at fabrics and patterns.

"Can we?" I asked again.

"We'll see. Maybe after."

First we searched the pattern books for a dress we

both liked. I didn't like anything. It's hard to tell from pictures in pattern books.

Finally my mother picked out a dress with puffy sleeves and a round neckline.

"What do you think?" she asked.

"You know how I hate puffy sleeves."

"Why? They're pretty. Soft-looking."

I shrugged.

"I can make the sleeves less puffy if you want."

I shrugged again. I could see I was getting on her nerves. "Okay, fine. Can we go for the grilled cheese now? We can pick out the fabric another time."

"We might as well look while we're here," she said.

I'm glad Aunt Esther wanted a blue wedding. I love blue. It's my favorite color. After lots of touching, feeling, comparing shades and prices, we chose a sky blue taffeta.

"Very dressy. And elegant," my mother said.

"Can we go eat now?" I asked.

"It's almost supper time. And besides, I can make you a grilled cheese sandwich and chocolate milk better and cheaper at home."

"I can't wait that long. I'm really hungry. I think I'm going to faint."

"I doubt that," my mother said. But off we went to Woolworth's and sat down at the counter. For me we ordered grilled cheese and a large chocolate milk. One of the best combinations in the world.

My mother ordered coffee for herself. She waited for it to cool off, took a few sips, and then we left.

When I came home from school a few days later, I was greeted by the sound of the sewing machine. Oh no! I knew what that meant.

My mother looked up from the machine when I came into the dining room.

"Hi, Dorrie. You're just in time to try this on."

"I really can't now, Ma. I've got a test in fractions that I've got to study for."

"It'll just take a minute."

A minute my eye. I knew that a half hour was more like it.

"So go ahead and take your clothes off. The sooner we start the sooner we'll finish."

"What about Artie? He'll walk in and see me in my underwear."

"Artie's staying late for basketball practice."

Sometimes I forgot that Artie was in high school and usually got home later than I did.

So I got undressed, climbed up on a chair in front of the mirror, and stood as still as I could while my mother pinned and measured and pinned again. Everything itched. I scratched. My whole body felt stiff. I stretched.

"Please stand still, Dorrie," my mother said. "You'll fall off the chair. And you need to stand still so I can get the measurements right."

"Look at me," I said, pointing to the mirror. "Look at how my collarbone sticks out. This dress will never look as good on me as it does in the picture."

"Wait until it's finished. It will look every bit as good," she said.

Fifteen minutes later I was free. But at eleven that night I woke up to the hum of the sewing machine. I got out of bed and went into the dining room. My mother was hunched over the sewing machine, concentrating hard.

"You're up late," I said.

"I'm having trouble with the sleeves."

"Can I get you something to drink?" I asked.

"No thanks. I'll be going to bed soon."

I stood behind her with my hands on her shoulders, watching her magic hands at work. She turned around, looked up at me, and smiled.

"You are going to look so beautiful," she said.

I knew that my mother was really working hard, sewing my dress and Victor's bedspread and getting the apartment all nice for him. But I really needed her help in deciding what to make for Sweet Semester.

"Ma," I said. "Sweet Semester is coming up pretty soon. And that Estelle Goodman is making taffy apples. Now what am I supposed to do?"

"I thought you were going to make caramel apples."

"They're practically the same thing. I need to make something else."

"Oh, Dorrie, this is not a good time to think about it. I've got your dress and mine to work on, and I have to get ready for Passover next week. What's the rush anyway? You have until June. And I'm really busy right now."

"You're always busy," I said. And I went back to bed.

Even though Passover is my favorite holiday and I always look forward to it, I knew that after it was over, there would be other reasons why she couldn't help me.

Victor was coming in, Aunt Esther was getting married . . .

There would never be a good time.

CHAPTER EIGHTEEN

Passover

Right before Passover the whole apartment was turned even more upside down. My father was now painting the bathroom so it would be nice for Victor. And my mother, in preparing for the holiday, was attacking the kitchen, wiping away all traces of food crumbs from the cupboards and stove and the Frigidaire.

Everything had to be clean. And special. Special dishes, special pots and pans and special foods. Everything separate from the rest of the year.

Artie and I schlepped the dishes and pots from the shed in the basement to our apartment on the first floor. The shed was dark and scary and I never went into it without Artie. He didn't like being there either.

"This place gives me the creeps," he said.

The order from the grocery store arrived in a big brown

cardboard box: matzo, nuts, raisins, macaroons, coffee, tea, dried apricots, sugar, and spices. My mother cooked—gefilte fish, chicken, and soup, and the relatives came to sit around the table and celebrate at the seder with us.

The seder was like every other seder we've ever celebrated. We drank wine and grape juice, and ate matzo instead of bread. We sang songs and read from the Haggadah (compliments of Maxwell House coffee), the book that tells the story of how the Jews were slaves in Egypt and how God brought us out and delivered us to freedom.

But the seder meant even more to us this year, my father was saying, because of Victor, who was coming out of his own slavery in Europe to live in freedom here with us.

"In every generation there have been those who tried to destroy us," he said. "And just as we were delivered from Egypt over three thousand years ago, now we have been delivered from Hitler—may his name be erased. Though he tried to annihilate us, we are still here."

"May we always be," said Bubbie.

And everyone answered, "Amen."

Over sponge cake and tea Uncle Louie told us that something else was special this Passover. He was back in business! He took over a kosher deli nearby on Roosevelt

Road. Roosevelt Road, where streetcars run along tracks on a street paved with cobblestones, where people in the neighborhood do most of their shopping.

"Mazel tov, mazel tov." We raised glasses and teacups. "Good luck to you. It's a wonderful deli in a wonderful location."

"Deli" is short for "delicatessen." Uncle Louie told us that the guy who owned it is retiring to California. Actually, the store is part deli and part restaurant, because you can buy stuff like corned beef, salami, and potato salad to take home, or you can eat at one of the tables in the back of the store. It also has a room for private parties.

The deli is called "Solly's," and Uncle Louie is going to keep the name because it's such a popular place. But when people get to know him he might change the name to "Louie's."

I'm very excited that an uncle of mine will be the owner of a deli. Uncle Louie was excited too.

"Now I don't have to worry about an A&P moving in," he said. "Ten of them can move in for all I care."

He promised that just as soon as he learned the business he'd invite all the relatives to a big celebration party where we'd be treated to anything we want.

My father was thrilled to hear that. He loves eating at

delis. He especially loves thick hot pastrami sandwiches on rye. I knew that even my mother would celebrate with us and not talk about how she can make better pastrami sandwiches at home.

I wondered if Victor would be here by then. I wondered if he'd ever eaten pastrami sandwiches.

Shortly after Passover, when April turned into May, Uncle Jack took a train to New York to pick Victor up. Then they would both take a train back together.

"Why don't you drive your '41 Plymouth?" I asked him before he left.

"I'm not sure the car would make it that far," he said. "Anyway, this will be a good time for Victor and me to get to know each other."

I kept thinking about Victor. And not just because he would be taking over my room. But I kept wondering: What will he look like? Will he be sad and scared? Will he like me? And how will we be able to understand each other? My mother told me that as far as she knew he could speak Yiddish and Polish and Russian. So maybe I'd be able to understand him if he spoke to me in Yiddish. But how would he be able to understand me?

I was thinking not only about Victor, but also about Aunt Esther. She was getting married in a month. Everyone went around saying, "Can you believe? It's almost June already. My how time flies."

I didn't want time to fly if that meant Aunt Esther would be moving away.

"I wish Aunt Esther and George would live here and not move to Minneapolis," I told my mother one day. She was basting the hem on my junior bridesmaid dress and I was trying to stand straight and still so I wouldn't get stuck with pins. "I wish Aunt Esther would stay here like always. Now I'll hardly ever see her."

My mother took a pin out of her mouth. "Nothing stays the same, Dorrie," she said. "Life moves on."

CHAPTER NINETEEN

Victor Arrives

When Victor arrived, Uncle Jack took him straight to Bubbie's house. We were going to meet him when we went there for dinner. While Victor was getting settled, Uncle Jack came over and told us a little about Victor's life during the war.

"We really got to know each other on that train ride," he said over a cup of coffee. "It's hard to imagine what that boy went through." And he went on to tell us how Victor and his family—his mother, father, and grandmother— and thousands of other Jews from Kovno were rounded up by the Germans and forced to live in a ghetto.

"The ghetto was surrounded by barbed wire." Uncle Jack said. "No running water, very little food. People were starving. Victor, Mina and Joseph, and Sophie were crowded into just two rooms with another family of four."

"Imagine," my mother said, shaking her head. "Eight people in two rooms."

"The family had a boy, David, who was a few years older than Victor. The two boys found a place where the wire around the ghetto had been cut, and they managed to sneak out to search for food to bring back. Victor told me he once bartered his watch for a couple of potatoes."

"A watch for potatoes?" Artie said as he fingered his own watch.

"One time after a few days of being away searching, Victor and David came back to find their families gone," Uncle Jack continued. "So the boys fled the ghetto and ran into the forest."

"What happened to their families?" I asked.

"Well, this is the saddest part," said Uncle Jack. "I don't even know how to tell it. And Victor only learned about it much later.

"It seems that when the Germans came to round up people for deportation to concentration camps, both families, along with lots of others, hid in underground hideouts—bunkers—that were scattered around the camp. But they were discovered … and …" He pushed his coffee cup away. "They were shot."

"Oh, my God," my mother gasped. Tears streamed down her face.

"A nightmare," my father murmured, placing his hand on hers.

A chill ran through me. Poor Victor, I thought. He's only sixteen years old. Just two years older than Artie. Five years (in June) older than me. And just like Uncle Jack said, I couldn't even begin to imagine all the things that had happened to him.

CHAPTER TWENTY

We Meet Victor

When we were getting ready to leave for Bubbie's house, I was so nervous I put on two mismatched shoes.

My whole family was nervous. Artie put way too much Brylcreem on his hair and it took two washings to get it all off.

My father lit up a cigarette and put it out when he remembered that he didn't smoke anymore.

And my mother kept giving us advice. "Now don't pry. Don't ask Victor any questions. If he wants to talk, he'll talk."

But I had questions. How and where did he hide from the Germans? What did he eat? How did he keep warm during the winter? Where did he sleep? And when I thought of that question, I had a question for myself. How could I begrudge him a nice warm place to sleep for two months when I had a nice warm place to sleep for almost eleven years?

I had questions.

It was Victor who opened the door. He smiled and greeted each of us by name and with a hug. Even though *he* was smiling, when he hugged me and said, "Dorrie," tears came to my eyes.

Bubbie, Uncle Jack, Aunt Esther, and George joined us. Buddy, too. Then we all went into the front room together.

Victor is tall and thin, with light brown hair and those blue cornflower eyes, just like Bubbie's. He sat in one of Bubbie's overstuffed chairs, with Buddy at his feet. It was as if Buddy knew that Victor needed special attention.

At first Victor didn't talk about the war or his family. He just talked about his trip by boat and how excited he was when he first saw the Statue of Liberty—which he called the Lady of Liberty—and the New York skyline.

"Everything was very beautiful. And the buildings—I never saw such tall buildings. And I thought, ah, so this is America. But where are the cowboys? I always heard there were cowboys in America."

Victor laughed when he said that and we all laughed with him. Then Artie said, "Hey, maybe we can take a trip out west and actually see some real cowboys."

"Yeah, let's do that," I said. "Can we? Can we go west for our vacation this summer?" I asked my mother and father.

And my father said, "Maybe we could. It's something to think about."

By then everyone seemed to be more comfortable with Victor. At least I was. And even though he spoke with an accent that made him sound like a young Uncle Louie, I understood everything he said because he spoke mostly in English, with Yiddish sprinkled in between some of the words.

"Where did you learn English?" I asked him. I looked at my mother to make sure the question I asked was okay. I don't know if she heard me or not because she didn't say anything. She kept her eyes on Victor the whole time.

"I learned after the war," Victor said. "In the DP camp. We had classes in English. But I hope to learn more now that I am here. With your help."

After a while we all went into the dining room for dinner. You could tell this dinner was special because the table was set with Bubbie's pink flowered dishes and napkins folded in triangles. And she was using her company glasses. Not the everyday tumblers. Those tumblers come with candles inside. They're memorial candles that you light each year on the date that a relative died. Then you wash out the glass and use it for drinking. Bubbie has a whole collection of them to go with her dishes from Dish Night.

Bubbie served chicken soup, roast chicken, brisket, and stuffed cabbage. Victor's face lit up when he saw everything.

"This is such a feast! And stuffed cabbage. Many times my mother made this for me. She knew it was my favorite food."

It got very quiet, and for a moment I didn't know who was going to cry first: Bubbie, or Victor, or my mother. But before anyone had a chance, my mother said, "Stuffed cabbage is a favorite of Dorrie's, too. Now I know for sure you two are related."

During the meal, little by little we found out a few more things about what happened to Victor and David after they escaped to the forest.

"When it got too cold outside we found places on farms. We hid in barns, under the hay."

"Did the farmers know you were there?" we wanted to know.

"Some did. One farmer here, one farmer there. They would let us hide in their barns. Sometimes for a few days, sometimes a few weeks. But then we had to leave. If their neighbors found out about us they would report us—and the farmers—to the Germans. But most of the time nobody knew. And we never stayed long in one place. We did not know who to trust."

Buddy came over and rested his chin on Victor's lap. And I tried to imagine what I would do if I had to hide from someone. Who could I trust? Where would I go? There are no forests or barns in my neighborhood. Where would I hide? In the basement? In the dark and spooky shed? I wrapped my arms around myself to keep from shivering.

"But Victor, what did you do for food?" This time I didn't even look at my mother before I asked the question.

Victor put his fork down on his plate. "We hid in the day, and at night we went to look for food. We always looked for what to eat. A turnip, a …how you call it …*kartoffel* …"

"A potato," I said.

"Yes, potato. And on the trees in the forest there were berries. Always we were hungry."

Bubbie gave him another cabbage roll. My father poured him another glass of ginger ale.

I looked at all the food on the table. And I thought of all the food we had on Rosh Hashanah and Passover. Even during the war, when certain foods were rationed, we always had enough to eat. Victor would probably have gobbled up my oatmeal. He would have drunk every drop of that guggle muggle. How could Sunny and I have ever thought we were suffering because we couldn't get any Fleer Dubble Bubble Gum?

"And here is a funny story for you," said Victor as he was finishing his meal. "One time we found a barn to hide in. But there was already a man hiding there. We wanted to hide with him, but he snored so loud ..." And here Victor stopped to make funny snoring sounds, laughing as he demonstrated.

"The whole barn shook," he continued. "We knew we had to get away fast!" And we laughed with Victor as he told the story.

"We lived that way for almost a year," Victor went on. "We lived through the war. We were lucky. And when the war was over, we found the DP camp. In Landsberg."

When Victor stopped to take a drink of ginger ale I thought that maybe he was finished talking. But he continued.

"In the DP camp I met a man I knew. He was from my town. From Kovno. He told me what happened to my family in the ghetto. From this man I learned ... my mother, my father, my grandmother—they were not so lucky."

Victor's eyes became misty. Nobody knew what to say. So we just sat there quietly, trying to finish our dinner.

"I saw a newsreel once," I finally said to break up the quiet. "'The Eyes and Ears of the World.' It showed how after the war, American soldiers riding in jeeps went through towns in Italy, or maybe France, tossing chocolate bars to the people who were lining the streets, cheering them."

"Nobody threw chocolate bars to us," said Victor. "Your package was the first time that I had chocolate in a long time. And the cookies! They brought back such wonderful memories of my family's bakery. I could almost taste the chocolate torte my grandmother used to make."

Just after he said that, Bubbie left the table and came back with—a chocolate torte! She presented it to Victor on a doily-covered plate, and oh my gosh, lying across the top of the torte was a single red rose. "Now that you are here you can have all the chocolate you want," she told him.

When Victor saw the familiar cake, a smile spread across his face. "Ah, this is so wonderful! But I think it would be too much even for me. Let us all enjoy it together."

While Bubbie sliced the torte, Artie asked, "What happened to David?"

"He is still in the DP camp, waiting. Waiting to go to Palestine."

We ate the torte down to the very last crumb. Then Bubbie showed Victor the recipe for the torte, written in his grandmother's handwriting. He studied it long and hard.

And I finally understood why Bubbie cried over the recipe that Sunday morning.

How to Make Bubbie's
(and Victor's Grandmother's)
Chocolate Nut Torte

INGREDIENTS

1 cup unsalted butter or
vegetable shortening
1 cup sugar, divided
6 eggs, separated

1 teaspoon vanilla extract
8 ounces bittersweet chocolate
1 cup finely ground almonds
1/4 cup finely ground hazelnuts

WHAT TO DO

Preheat oven to 350°. Lightly grease a 9-inch springform pan. Line bottom with wax paper and lightly grease.

Melt butter and chocolate in a double boiler. In a large bowl beat egg yolks with 1/2 cup sugar until thick and creamy. Add vanilla and chocolate mixture. Stir in nuts.

In a separate bowl whisk egg whites to form soft peaks. Gradually add remaining 1/2 cup sugar and whisk until peaks become stiff but not dry. Fold a small amount into chocolate mixture to loosen it. Fold remaining egg whites until just combined.

Pour batter into pan. Bake for about 50-55 minutes or until a toothpick comes out with a few moist crumbs. Let cool.

Remove side pan. Invert cake so the bottom becomes the top. Remove bottom pan and wax paper.

Top with powdered sugar, or whipped cream and strawberries. Serve at room temperature or chilled.

Note: Most of the time you don't want your cakes to fall. But this torte is supposed to fall. So when it caves in and cracks don't worry. Later when you turn it over it will look beautiful!

CHAPTER TWENTY-ONE

Hot Fudge Sundaes

Over the next couple of weeks we showed Victor all around Chicago: the museums, the zoos, the Art Institute. We even showed him Montrose Beach, where we'll be spending most of our summer Sundays.

One day my father came home early from work and he took Victor out to buy him a suit for Aunt Esther's wedding. Artie already had his suit from Passover.

Victor looked so happy when he got back. "The suit is a nice dark blue," he said to me. "With pencil stripes."

"Pencil stripes?" I asked.

"Yes. Pencil stripes." And he made a motion of drawing vertical stripes down his shirt.

"Oh, you mean pinstripes," I told him.

"Pinstripes. Yes. I will show you when it comes back from the tailor."

And then when I saw how happy he was sharing my room with Artie, I didn't mind so much that I was in the dining room. But I still wasn't comfortable there, and sometimes I felt like I was on display in a store window. There was this one morning when our neighbor, Mrs. Kaluky, came in from across the hall to ask for my mother's help. She needed to let out a few seams from a dress.

"I'm getting so big I look like a house and a lot," she told my mother. And when they came into the dining room to work on the dress, I stuck my head under the new summer quilt my mother made for me and hid there until she left.

My mother then joined me on the couch with her recipe box.

"I've been thinking about some things you can make for Sweet Semester," she said. "How about baking a carrot cake. I can show you how."

"A carrot cake?"

"I know it's not one of your favorites, but people seem to like it."

"Not kids."

"Then how about blueberry muffins," she said, flipping through the cards.

"I was hoping for something chocolate," I told her.

"Then we can make an easy basic chocolate cake," she said, still flipping.

"Boring."

"Oh, I have something here. A banana cake. We could make it chocolate."

"Rosalyn Russo hates bananas. She wouldn't vote for it."

"Brownies, then. Kids like brownies. And you already know how to make them."

"Somebody's already doing brownies."

I looked through the recipes with her. Some of them seemed kind of hard. I thought I'd better not experiment. Better not take a chance.

"You know what, Ma? Maybe I'll just stick with the chocolate caramel apples. I know they'll come out good. But thanks anyway."

"What about Estelle Goodman?" she asked, closing up the box.

"Her apples will be taffy. Mine will be caramel. And chocolate."

One Sunday my father took Artie, Victor, and me to Ye Olde Chocolate Shoppe on Roosevelt Road to get hot fudge sundaes. We sat at a small round table and waited for the waitress to bring them. I love hot fudge sundaes. Especially the ones I get from Ye Olde Chocolate Shop. The ice cream is topped with a mountain of whipped cream and nuts and a cherry, and here's the best part—the hot fudge comes in a small glass pitcher. You get your very own pitcher. And you can be the one to decide where you want to pour the fudge. Nobody else pours it for you. It's a wonderful experience.

I poured the fudge onto the whipped cream in the shape of a flower. The fudge reminded me of melted caramel.

"For Sweet Semester I've decided to make chocolate caramel apples," I told everyone. "It won't be the most original, but I can't think of anything better and I'm just not going to worry about it anymore."

"I still think you should make a marshmallow snowman," Artie said.

"What is Sweet Semester?" Victor asked.

When I explained it to him he just nodded. Well, I thought, he has more important things to think about than a dessert contest. There were times I would see him just staring into space. Maybe he was thinking his private thoughts. Maybe he was just staring. I'll never know.

How to Make a Hot Fudge Sundae

INGREDIENTS

fudge
1 or 2 scoops of vanilla ice cream
whipped cream

finely chopped nuts
maraschino cherry

WHAT TO DO

Melt fudge in a bowl over simmering water.
Place 1 or 2 scoops of vanilla ice cream in a sundae dish.*
Top with whipped cream, finely chopped nuts, and a maraschino cherry.
Pour the fudge over the top of the whipped cream.

If you use a small glass pitcher for the fudge, you will have a sundae that looks just like the one at Ye Olde Chocolate Shoppe.

*Note that I say to use vanilla ice cream. This is my one exception to chocolate. And that's because the chocolate fudge looks beautiful over the lovely white whipped cream and vanilla ice cream.

CHAPTER TWENTY-TWO

A Private Party and a Wedding

One of the best things we did took place on my birthday, June 10. We celebrated the official grand opening of Solly's, Uncle Louie's new deli.

When I asked my mother, "Do you think Uncle Louie will mind if I ask Sunny to come to the grand opening with us?" she said, "I'm sure he'll be happy to have someone who has such fine character."

The store was closed to regular customers. Even the sign on the window said so:

CLOSED DUE TO PRIVATE PARTY!!

All my relatives—on both sides of the family—were there. A few of Uncle Louie's friends were there too. But mostly it was family. Aunt Goldie acted as the official hostess who stood at the door to welcome us. She kissed Artie, Victor, and me, and even Sunny. "Sit wherever you like," she said. "Order whatever you like. Don't be bashful."

We sat down at a cozy table at the very back of the private room reserved especially for parties, and right away we started eating the half-sour pickles that swam in a small barrel in the middle of the table. When the waiter came over with the menus, Victor said, "There is so much to choose from. I do not know what to get."

Artie made a suggestion. "Let's start with hot dogs and go from there." So we ordered four hot dogs with the works: mustard, onions, relish, and tomatoes, and French fries. We washed it down with cream sodas. Then we ordered thick hot corned beef sandwiches on rye and more cream sodas.

I found a beautiful slice of corned beef in my sandwich that looked like a tongue. So I let it hang out of my mouth and said, "Look, I'm a cow."

Artie and Victor laughed, and Sunny started mooing. Nobody else seemed to notice.

Music from a phonograph played all evening. Everyone was having a good time, eating, talking, and laughing. My father gave a toast to Uncle Louie and Aunt Goldie. "To much success." And to Victor, "We are so happy to have you with us."

And before I knew it, a waiter was bringing a huge chocolate sheet cake topped with twelve sparkling candles (eleven and one for good luck) to my table, and everyone burst into song. "Happy Birthday to you, happy birthday to you, happy birthday, dear Dorrie …"

I made a wish and blew out the candles. Then I looked around the room at my mother and father, Bubbie, Uncle Jack, Aunt Esther and George, Uncle Louie and Aunt Goldie, Artie and Victor, and so many other relatives. And of course, there was my friend Sunny. All of them were smiling at me, making me feel warm and happy inside.

Aunt Esther's wedding took place a few days later and it was beautiful. I didn't trip down the aisle or anything, and I got to wear a corsage of white gardenias on my dress. The dress really looked pretty, even with the puffy sleeves. I just know this dress was prettier than any I could ever buy in a store. And it was one of a kind. Made especially for me by my mother.

When Bubbie saw me in the dress for the first time and saw my hair worn down with rhinestone barrettes to keep it in place, she gave me a big smile and said, "Hoo ha!" That was the best compliment I could ever get. But I was happiest for Victor in his new blue suit with the pencil stripes.

"You look so handsome," I told him.

"The suit—it fits good?" he asked, smoothing down the sleeves.

"It's perfect," I said. And he gave me the biggest smile. Then he spun around and performed a little tap dance that made us both laugh.

"You're a regular Fred Astaire," I told him.

"Who is this Fred Astaire?"

"Only the most famous dancer in Hollywood."

"Ah, in that case, come," he said. And he took my hand and led me onto the dance floor.

Jeepers! We were going to dance? What did I know about dancing? Except for dancing with Artie when he needed me to practice with him for a party, and way, way back, dancing with my father, my small feet on his big shoes, what did I know about dancing?

And yet, there we were, Dorrie Meyers and Fred Astaire swaying gently to "Moonlight Serenade." We moved lightly to the music, both of us laughing when Victor twirled me around. He was so elegant. And when I looked up at him to ask where he learned to dance so well, he just looked down at me and smiled. It was so good to see him happy, I never even asked.

Too soon the music and dancing were over and we

went back to our table. My father, as usual, gave a toast. "To Esther and George. May you share many happy years together. *L'chaim*." (That means "to life.")

After the dinner a sweet table was set up with all kinds of cakes and cookies and fruit. But I think the best things were the miniature chocolate éclairs. I ate some there and took some home. They were delicious. They would have been spectacular for Sweet Semester had I known how to make them. Oh well.

CHAPTER TWENTY—THREE

Sweet Semester, 1946

It was a few days before school let out and I was getting ready to make the chocolate caramel apples. Victor volunteered to go out to buy the caramels. He wanted to get to know the neighborhood by himself.

I was busy washing and drying the apples when he returned with a large bag that he set on the kitchen table. I couldn't understand why the grocer would put a batch of caramels into such a large bag.

"Thank you for the caramels," I said to Victor.

"I did not buy caramels for you," he said.

"How come, Victor? Were they out of them?"

"I bought you something else. You do not have to make caramel apples." He turned the bag over and spilled out tons of peppermint candy sticks, along with cans of coconut shreds and bags of chocolate chips.

"You can make something I am sure nobody else will make. They are called peppermint chocolate sticks. In my family's bakery we also made candy. This is my favorite. It is also the only candy I remember how to make. It is very easy.

"First you have to ... to ... how you say ... *tzeshmetter* the candy."

"Tze what?" I asked. It was a word I had never heard before.

Victor found my mother's rolling pin, put the peppermint sticks into a paper bag, and started to smash them into little pieces.

"Oh, you mean you have to smash the candy?"

"Yes. You smash the candy."

"Okay, I get it." And I took the rolling pin and tzeshmettered the rest of the sticks into tiny pieces.

Victor directed as I melted the chocolate and added the crushed candies and coconut shreds. Then I spread the mixture onto wax paper in the shape of a rectangle and waited for it to get firm in the Frigidaire. When it did I took a knife and cut it into sticks. And behold! Peppermint chocolate sticks. Victor and I each sampled a stick. It was so wonderful that

I gave Victor a great big hug. "Thank you, Victor. You saved me."

"I thank you," he said. "You brought back happy memories for me. Sweet memories."

Later on my mother and father and Artie each tasted a stick.

"These are great," said Artie. "And I have to admit, they're even better than my marshmallow snowman."

My mother said they were so good that she would make them for the girls the next time they came over to play bridge. And I had to keep an eye out to make sure my father didn't snitch any when I wasn't looking. I needed them for Sweet Semester the next day.

I also needed my essay about Victor and the peppermint chocolate sticks. So I filled up my Esterbrook from my bottle of ink and began.

It was hard to know what to write. There was so much to tell. Should I just tell about Victor's life before the ghetto—the happy times—and leave out the really sad parts that came later? Or should I tell the whole story? And if Victor read my essay or heard it in class, how would it make him feel?

I stayed up late working, and little by little the words came.

On the morning of Sweet Semester, my mother took her time while she braided my hair and tied ribbons at the ends. And because today was a special day, and the photographer was coming, I let her do it.

The kids streamed into our spick-and-span classroom with their entries. They brought them in bags and boxes and in wax paper-covered packages tied together with string. Even Miss Fitzgerald came in with a box. Everyone was so excited. It was like we were at a birthday party and couldn't wait to see the presents. But we would have to wait until after lunch to see what we all brought and for the contest to begin.

I couldn't believe what was waiting for me when I came home for lunch. Right on the dining room table was a large envelope addressed to me from Margaret O'Brien at MGM Studios.

"She answered me! She answered me!" I shouted as I jumped up and down. "Whoopee!"

"What a nice surprise," my mother said, smiling.

I opened up the envelope to find a photograph of Margaret O'Brien signed to me.

To my friend Dorrie, Margaret O'Brien.
There was a letter, too.

> *Dear Dorrie,*
>
> *Thank you for your letter. And thank you for seeing my movies. It's fun being a movie star. I get to meet interesting people and work with a lot of great actors.*
>
> *If the parts I play seem real to you it's because I truly believe the role that I'm playing. And that makes it easy to cry when I have to.*
>
> *So if you believe what you write in your essay, you will do a good job reading it in front of your audience.*
>
> *I hope you win for Sweet Semester. And I hope you get your picture in the newspaper. Good luck!*
>
> *I think it's swell that your class is sending money to war orphans and hungry children.*
>
> *Your friend,*
> *Margaret O'Brien*

As my mother was reading the letter I started jumping up and down again.

"It was so nice of her to have answered you," she said.

"I didn't think she would. I have to show the letter to Sunny." I folded it up neatly and tucked it into the pocket of my blouse. Then I slipped the photo back into the envelope and placed it on the dining room table. I didn't want to take it to school and get it all messed up. I'd show it to Sunny later.

"What a great letter!" Sunny said as we were walking back to school. "You're so lucky."

"I hope the letter will bring us both luck," I told her.

It was just like a birthday party when we returned to the classroom. The two long tables that were in the back of the room were draped with white tablecloths and set with plates and trays of desserts. A number was placed in front of each dessert.

Everything was ready for tasting. The large cakes were cut into bite-size pieces, cupcakes were cut into quarters, and large cookies were broken in half. There were Estelle Goodman's taffy apples, too. They were cut into small pieces and starting to turn brown.

The only thing not cut up were these amazing painted Superman cookies displayed in the center of each table.

Superman, all red and blue, was in a flying position ready to take off.

"Wow!" was all anyone could say. And we all knew who had made those cookies. Melvin Freid. Now I was sure I didn't have any chance of winning.

Chairs were set up all around the room for the visitors. And there was coffee and tea for the adults.

On a nearby desk sat a large jar that looked like the kind that once held sour pickles, with a sign taped on it that said THANK YOU FOR CONTRIBUTING TO THE CHILDREN'S FOOD FUND.

"Look, there's money already in it," said Sunny, who was holding a bulging paper bag.

"I bet Miss Fitzgerald wanted to get the donations off to a good start," I said as I dropped in my Hanukkah silver dollar. "What's in the bag?"

Without a word Sunny opened up the bag, and when she turned it over, a stream of shiny silver pennies cascaded into the jar. After the other kids saw her do that they began dropping their money into the jar too.

The class settled down and as Miss Fitzgerald passed out the ballots for voting, she said, "Please note that the marble pound cake is mine and is not eligible for your vote."

As if I would ever vote for a pound cake.

"After you taste everything," she continued, "just write down the number of the dessert you like the most. You are not to vote for your own. And just take a little of anything that looks good to you. I don't want you to eat too much and get sick. Whatever is left over you can take back home."

As we began to sample the food, the guests came trickling in. Everyone dropped money into the food fund jar. I watched for my mother and Bubbie, who were coming with Victor. And I also watched for the reporter and photographer from the *Chicago Daily News*. I figured that the photographer would come in with a huge camera. Not just a Kodak Brownie. And the reporter would wear a hat with a card that said PRESS stuck in the hatband. Just like the reporters wear in the movies.

Sunny and I walked around together, filling our plates with s'mores and strawberry shortcake and cookies topped with Hershey kisses, and of course, my peppermint chocolate sticks. We ignored anything that didn't look good to us. Anything mushy or runny or all dried up.

Some kids ate Superman and others said he looked too good to eat and wanted to take him home. I ate one cookie and took one home to give to my father.

I was in the middle of tasting a piece of a blueberry muffin when someone tapped me on the shoulder. I turned around and saw Artie, who said he came to take pictures with his camera. But I think he really came to sample the desserts, because he started eating right away.

Pretty soon my mother and Bubbie and Victor walked in and I waved them over.

"My, my look at all these delicacies," my mother said.

"This is just like a bakery," said Victor.

And Bubbie said, "Hoo ha!" Then she poured herself a cup of coffee and took a peppermint stick.

Sunny's mother couldn't come to Sweet Semester because she had to work. So we kind of adopted Sunny for the afternoon.

First my mother dropped a couple of dollars into the jar and then went straight for Sunny's s'mores. "Sunny, this is wonderful. Better than any I have ever made," she told her. And Sunny's whole face lit up.

The kids seemed to like my peppermint chocolate sticks and took seconds and thirds, and a few of the teachers who came in to sample the food agreed that my peppermint chocolate sticks were delicious and refreshing. Maybe I did have a chance of winning after all.

Miss Fitzgerald welcomed the guests and thanked

them for coming to the annual Sweet Semester and contributing to the Children's Food Fund.

"Everyone, please fill up your plates, take a seat and enjoy," she said.

Then the kids voted for their favorite dessert. I voted for Superman. And I patted my Margaret O'Brien letter for good luck.

While we continued nibbling and listening to the essays being read, the photographer and reporter from the *Chicago Daily News* walked in. The photographer had his huge camera, but the reporter wasn't wearing a hat. He only had a small notebook with him.

Rosalyn Russo had the whole class laughing when she read her essay. She wrote that she baked a strawberry shortcake to make up for the birthday cake she never got to eat. It seems that when her mother was bringing in the cake, she tripped on the edge of the kitchen linoleum that her father forgot to tack down.

"She fell face-first into the cake," Rosalyn read. "And it was lucky for her that the candles blew out on the way down. And in the end the only one who got to taste the cake was my mother."

It was the funniest essay of the afternoon. And I just

knew Miss Fitzgerald would vote for hers because she was laughing so much when Rosalyn read it.

The room was totally quiet when I read my essay. I told about Victor who gave me the recipe for his favorite candy from his family's bakery before the war. Before the Germans took them away. I wrote about him hiding in barns and forests and living in a DP camp and being the only one in his family to survive.

"And when he watched me make the candy and tasted it, he said it brought back sweet memories of a happier time. And I'm hoping those happy memories will take away even a little bit of the sad ones."

While I was reading I glanced at Victor and saw him looking at me. And I hoped that what I read was okay with him.

A half hour before the bell rang for dismissal, Miss Fitzgerald was ready to announce the winners.

"First, for the most favorite dessert ..." I held my breath. "It was almost unanimous. The winner is ... Melvin Freid for his Superman cookies! They taste as wonderful as they look."

Everyone cheered and applauded Melvin. We all knew he would win.

"And now, for the best essay." I held my breath again and waited for her to announce Rosalyn's name.

"The winner is ... Dorrie Meyers!"

More cheers and applause. This time for me! I couldn't believe it. Sunny climbed out of her seat and gave me a standing ovation. My mother and Bubbie and Victor and Artie applauded like crazy.

And I couldn't believe it when she called Melvin and me up to the front of the room to accept our blue ribbons.

She pinned on Melvin's ribbon first. It said, "Sweet Semester 1946. First Place. Best Dessert."

And then she pinned on my ribbon. "Sweet Semester 1946. First Place. Best Essay."

The photographer took a picture of each of us, while the reporter wrote something down in his notebook.

"Okay," the photographer said, "now let's get a shot of the winners together."

I held up my hand and said, "Wait a second!" and ran over to where Victor was sitting. I grabbed his arm and pulled him up to the front of the room.

"Everybody," I announced, "this is Victor!"

The next evening I couldn't wait for my father to bring home the *Chicago Daily News*. So I ran out to

Ziffer's Drugstore to buy a copy. I searched through the paper while I was still in the store. And finally, there it was! Not on the front page, but not with the want ads or crossword puzzle either. Right on page seventeen was the heading:

LAWSON FIFTH GRADERS SHARE THEIR SWEET SEMESTER

WITH HUNGRY CHILDREN IN EUROPE

There was the story about Sweet Semester and how we collected almost forty dollars for the Children's Food Fund. Melvin's recipe was there and my recipe and essay too. And there were our pictures. One of Melvin, one of me, and one of Melvin, Victor, and me together. All of us wearing wide grins.

I couldn't be sure, but I think Victor's grin was the widest of all.

How to Make Victor's Peppermint Chocolate Sticks

INGREDIENTS

8 ounces chocolate chips
1/2 cup crushed peppermint
    candy sticks

1/4 cup shredded coconut

WHAT TO DO

Melt the chocolate in a double boiler.

Stir in the peppermint candies and coconut.

Spread the mixture over wax paper to make a rectangle about 5 x 8 inches.

Chill in refrigerator for 30 minutes.

With a sharp knife carefully cut into sticks about 2-1/2 inches long x 1/2 inch wide.

CHAPTER TWENTY-FOUR

Hello, Summer

It was the last day of school and we went in for just half a day.

We returned our fifth grade books, took down art-work and decorations, and washed the blackboards. And we received our report cards that told us we were promoted to sixth grade.

The room was clean and ready for the next fifth grad-ers to take our places and enjoy a Sweet Semester. I won-dered who would be sitting in my seat. I had hoped Miss Fitzgerald would make a surprise announcement and say that she was going to be our teacher in sixth grade, too. But she didn't.

Instead, she stood in front of the room and told us how much she liked all of us and what a pleasure it was to teach us and how she hoped her next class would be as wonderful.

All the classes filed silently and orderly out of the school, but as soon as we hit the streets we screamed and shouted and sang out, "School's out, school's out, teacher let the monkeys out!"

Sunny and I sat on the swings in the playground to compare report cards. We laughed when we saw what Miss Fitzgerald wrote in each one.

In Sunny's she wrote, "Sunny, it was a pleasure having you in my class. Please practice your spelling over the summer."

In mine she wrote, "Dorrie, it was a pleasure having you in my class. Please practice your arithmetic over the summer."

"I do not intend to spend my vacation practicing my spelling," said Sunny. "I just want to play and have fun."

"Me too," I said. "In fact, we're going out west to Texas for two weeks to visit the Alamo. Victor wants to see cowboys."

"You're going away for two weeks? What will I do without you?" Sunny asked. But after a moment she turned to me and smiled. "I guess that's all right. It'll be nice for Victor."

I put my arm around her and smiled back. "You know something, Sunny Shapiro? You are indeed a person of fine character."

Author's Note

Although *My Chocolate Year* is a work of fiction, the story was inspired by real people and my own experiences.

I grew up in Chicago in the 1940s just as Dorrie did. Like Dorrie, I wasn't much of a cook or baker, though my mother and *her* mother (my bubbie) were magicians in the kitchen. Bubbie never used a recipe because she couldn't read or write, and she enjoyed cooking and baking all of my favorite foods.

My father owned a mattress manufacturing company and always carried packs of gum in his jacket pockets. And my mother, like Dorrie's mother, sewed all of her clothes, and mine, and always said she could make any food better and cheaper at home. My brother, Irv, became Artie in the story. He enjoyed teasing me, but he was, and still is a very good brother.

My uncle Jack *did* have an English springer spaniel named Buddy, and to this day he loves to talk about his 1941 Plymouth. My Aunt Esther always made a big production out of getting ready for a date, and I loved following her around the house, watching as she took apart the closet in her search for something to wear.

Uncle Louie had a grocery store (but not a delicatessen, though I wished he did), and my mother always reminded us not to ask for anything when we went there to shop. But he gave us free candy bars anyway.

When I was growing up, the school year was divided into two semesters. The first semester ran from September until the end of January. The second semester went from February through June. Sometimes we changed rooms for each semester. And sometimes we even changed teachers.

I enjoyed going to the movies to see Margaret O'Brien who was a famous child actress in the 1940s. But Dorrie's and Margaret's letters to each other are only in my imagination.

We entertained ourselves with radio (very few people had television when this story takes place), and listened to all sorts of programs. There were soap operas like *Aunt Jenny* during the day, kids' shows like *Superman* and the

Lone Ranger after school, and family shows in the evenings. And everyone listened to the latest news about the war. (World War II ended in August of 1945, just before this story begins.)

Jewish families like mine, and like Dorrie's, gathered together during holidays where the topic of conversation usually centered around the war, and worry over the Jews who were being persecuted in Europe.

Victor was inspired by a neighbor's relative who was the sole Holocaust survivor in his family. He lived in a DP camp before coming to live in freedom here in America.

Charlotte Herman

About the Author and Illustrator

Charlotte Herman is the author of many beloved books for children, including the acclaimed Millie Cooper series and *The House on Walenska Street*. Like Dorrie, Charlotte possesses a lifelong love of family, chocolate malteds, and hot fudge sundaes. She makes her home outside of Chicago.

LeUyen Pham is the acclaimed illustrator of a number of books. She lives, works, and teaches in San Francisco, California.